I0631802

mayhem

chaos fuel
book one

Amy Booker

RENAISSAN
PUBLISHING
LIMITED

Mayhem

By

Amy Booker

Copyright © 2024 Amy Booker

All rights reserved. No parts of this book may be copied, distributed, or published in any form without express written permission from the publisher. Violators will be prosecuted to the fullest extent of the law. Plus, plagiarism and pirating are just ick. Do better.

For permissions, contact: amybookerauthor@gmail.com. I'll probably give it to you.

This novel is a work of fiction in which all events and characters in this book are the product of the author's crazy imagination. Locations may be familiar but are most likely twisted for artistic expression. Any resemblance to actual people is really freaking cool but entirely (usually) coincidental. While I did attend law school, I am not a lawyer, and nothing I write should be taken as legal advice. I take a lot of liberties with my dramatic license since it took me years to pass the written test. Also, if I reference a medical condition, I might have experience with it, so please know nothing in the world conforms to a single interpretation of reality. Everyone is afflicted and reacts to things differently, even with the same diagnosis.

Published by Renaissan Publishing Limited, Cuyahoga Falls, Ohio

www.amybookerauthor.com

author's note

If you've read my previous books, you'll know the chapter names are all song titles. Music has been an integral part of my life and always sets the mood for my writing. Whether it's the overall energy of a song, the lyrics, or even the title, that tone carries through into my written words on the page. The playlist and a link can be found at the back of each book, or you can find them on my website: www.amybookerauthor.com.

When chaos swirls around you,
its traitorous roots taking hold,
don't give up or give in.
Thrive, darling.
Thrive.

one
numb

Brad

The politics of rock 'n roll fucking suck. And it's not just the kissing asses and kissing babies part of it to keep our 'image' in check that rubs me the wrong way. It's the whole – 'be somebody you're not.' Because ultimately, that's exactly what it is.

'*Whatever it is you're doing, stop doing that. You should look like this, and sound like this, and act like this...*'

Fuck that noise.

I have never conformed to what society expected of me a day in my life, and I'm not inclined to start now. And while we're now sitting in the conference room of our record label getting our asses handed to us for losing another bass player, we got here by being ourselves in the first place. The suits never see that part of the equation.

Our new manager, Ian Summer, a former British rockstar himself, seems to get it. *Mostly*. And is trying to stick up for us.

"Eliza, you know that Frankie wasn't going to be able to cut it in the long run," he says to the VP of Blackmore Records, our label. "I say it's better that this happened now on the way up, rather than at the top, wouldn't you agree?"

The exec twirls a lock of hair as she considers his question, it's shoulder-length, and platinum with bright blue ends. At first glance, she's not your typical boardroom filler, but she can be a hardass when she wants. Unfortunately, it looks like she wants to be one right now.

Lucky us.

"I get what you're saying, Ian. I do." She glances around at us, a bit disparagingly. "But Frankie was the third bass player this year alone. And these people have contracts that we need to pay out, even when they leave. We can't afford to keep doing this."

And there it is. It's all about the money. It always is. We're digging into their bottom line. Fuck the music. Fuck the artistry.

Money. Money. Money.

Ian nods and rubs a hand down his face as if he understands. Before managing us, he was an executive with Blackmore too. In fact, he's the guy that got us signed with the label in the first place. But he's a former musician. He gets where we're coming from. I really hope he's not about to start agreeing that we need to change somehow, because that would piss me the fuck off. I like Ian, and I don't want that to change over this stupid shit.

Band members come and go all the time, and all over the place. Hell, I couldn't even count the number of bands I've been in and left for one reason or another. Sure, not always by my choice, but that's how it is. Everything in this business is temporary, except the music.

The music is what fucking matters.

"So, what are the options, then?" Ian asks, his eyes tired. "I take it you have a suggestion as to how to fix this?"

Eliza looks around at all of us, her face unreadable. But I get the sense that she's trying to figure out how we're going to react to whatever she's about to say. My spine tingles with fight or flight reactions at the ready.

"Your auditions for a new bass player start next week, correct?" She asks, but she knows the answer already. I'm not crazy about the slight nervousness in her tone now. As if she knows she's about to disappoint us. When we only nod, she goes on. "Well, we've brought in a new PR person for the label, Tess Lagerfeld. She's brilliant at image makeovers. A little new at this industry, but she's a game changer. And she'll be shadowing you during the process and handling all social media going forward for Chaos Fuel."

We all stare at each other, dumbfounded.

'Image makeover?'

Oh, fuck this.

two
rock show

Tess

W hen Eliza Kerr invited me to work for Blackmore Records, I was initially hesitant. Music PR isn't my wheelhouse. Believe it or not, it's a completely different skillset from working with actors or politicians, who, amazingly, are very similar in their public relations nightmares. And technically, are easier to put a shine on.

Music fans are a little more nuanced than a typical audience because music itself speaks to the soul, not the mind. Lyrics and melodies call to a person's heart and live there. Once that gets tarnished, it's a lot harder to polish.

I welcome the challenge that this will bring, but I am not one to jump ships like this. I liked the stability of my previous jobs. I knew what to expect from day to day. I needed that control in my life. Ever since my parents divorced when I was young, and I bounced between houses I've craved order.

So, why I accepted Eliza's offer, I have no idea. The

only reason I can come up with is that I'd hit a mental plateau of some kind. Nothing felt fulfilling anymore. There wasn't any purpose to anything, other than to do the same thing over and over. Rinse and repeat.

I was bored.

Chaos Fuel will be my first project with Blackmore, and in my research of the current state of their PR, it's going to be a complete trial by fire. They've fired every manager they've had except the current one (so far). They can't keep a bass player to save their lives. Brad Chambers, the singer, is known to be a playboy, though that's slowed down a little bit the last few years. Emmett Cavenaugh, the drummer, is a horrible prankster that nobody wants to work with. And Stefan Karlsson, their guitarist, parties way too much.

Typical rockstars.

Brad is the one that stands out for me, and not just because he's the incredibly hot lead singer with a voice of an angel who smokes menthols; He's a dad. He has an eight-year-old daughter, Charlotte, he shares with an ex who is married to the bass player of Indigo King, another Blackmore Records band.

While Chaos Fuel may be typical rockstars, with typical bad boy reputations – full of too much partying, hot lingerie models, and every other excess imaginable - fixing their image won't be so easy. The press seems to always want to find the flaws, and never look at the good stuff. So, researching anything good about the band is almost impossible. Outside of Blackmore's own press releases, there isn't a lot to work with. Everything positive comes from the fans themselves.

That's got to be my angle - the connection between the band and the fans. But to do that, I'm going to need to see them in action. And that means I need to meet them. Soon.

Eliza told me that the band will be holding auditions for a new bass player next week, so that's my opportunity to get up close and personal and get an idea of what I'm working with. I won't know how to approach any of this if I don't know them.

Chaos Fuel, here I come.

what a wonderful world

Brad

"But Jude said I could," my eight-year-old daughter, Charlie says, opening the fridge in my apartment, looking for a soda. Something I purposely don't have for a very good reason. Charlotte on concentrated sugar isn't something anyone wants to deal with.

"Well, that's awesome for him," I say, not sure if I don't believe Jude would say that just to get at me. He's married to my ex, and Charlotte's mother, Ren, and we haven't always seen eye-to-eye on things. We play it cool for Charlie's sake, though.

They're both off to London for six weeks with their youngest child – son August, since Indigo King are judges for some TV rock band talent show that I've never heard of, and Charlie didn't want to go. So, I get to spend some quality time with my girl. I was over the moon when she said she wanted to hang with me instead of taking the trip overseas.

But now I need to entertain an eight-year-old little girl.

We have gigs still on the schedule in a few weeks, but they're up in the air without us having a permanent bass player in place. The upcoming auditions are even more pressing now than before Eliza's lecture, with those dates looming.

"You don't have any soda," Charlie announces, obviously disappointed, crossing her arms over her chest, her long red curls just like her mother's bounce as she huffs.

"I never said I did."

"But Jude said I could have some," She repeats. Her lower lip is now making a bold appearance in her growing pout.

"Well, then Jude should have given it to you and not assumed I had any," I shrug, keeping my face impassive. "There's always water. Or beer."

Charlie's a smart girl. She's not usually difficult, and her sense of humor is sharper than most. At my suggestion of beer her pout twitches briefly before she breaks out in laughter.

"You're silly," she says between giggles. "I can't drink beer until next year when I'm twenty-one."

I smack my forehead. "Oh, that's right. I keep forgetting you're not middle-aged yet."

Still giggling, she throws herself onto the couch. "And you're out of beer too."

"Well, damn," I groan, pretending to be upset. "I guess we're both out of luck, huh?"

She turns serious again. "So, are we going to do anything fun while I'm here?"

I'm not sure how to take her question. I think we have fun every time we get together. Not that I try to be the 'fun' dad who entertains her every second, but I try to make the most of our time. However, when this stay was planned months ago, I didn't realize I'd have to spend any of it looking for a new bass player. That's not something I'd categorize as 'fun.'

"Well, you're going to help Chaos Fuel pick out a new bass player. That'll be cool, right?"

Her eyes go wide. "Really? I can pick?"

"No, you can *help* us pick."

She seems to be transported into a dream world. "What if they're all like, really cute? I won't be able to pick."

A chuckle bubbles up, and I shake my head. "Yeah, that's always the hard part. What if they're all really cute?"

The size of the eyeroll that remark gets me has to hurt. How does she do that? "Dad, they *have* to be cute to be in your band. It's important."

This surprises me. "Oh? And why is that?" Here I thought it was our music that mattered. Silly me. Maybe Charlie could be our new PR rep instead of this Tess person.

"Because," she sighs dramatically, "if you want girls to like your music, you have to be cute."

I arch a brow at her. "And who told you that?"

"Well, it's just my opinion. But everyone thinks that

way." She shrugs matter-of-factly, but I see a hint of doubt flash in her eyes.

I love that doubt. She *should* doubt that opinion.

"And do you always do what everybody else does?"

She scrunches her nose at the idea.

There's my girl.

"No." Her forehead creases as she clearly starts to examine her position on the matter.

I don't continue and let her figure out how she wants to deal with this personal revelation. Some things just need to be figured out on their own without intervention.

I'm not a candidate for 'Dad of the year.' Never have been. In fact, in the very beginning, I was downright awful. I was scared shitless to become a dad; thinking it would ruin my life, and crush my music dreams, hold me back somehow.

The exact opposite is true.

Having Charlie in my life has changed me so completely, it's mind blowing to look at how we started, to where we are now. Never in my wildest dreams did I think I could do both – and succeed at either of them. Not that I'm perfect. I'm not. I still have moments of my old mindset creep in on occasion and go off the rails a bit on some quest for 'freedom.' But overall, I think I'm doing okay with everything.

That's today's feeling. It can change in a heartbeat.

"Okay, he can be ugly," Charlie says ruefully, snapping me out of my reminiscence.

"Wow, Charlie. Really?" I say, not sure I like this opinion either.

"What?" Her bright eyes turn up to me questioningly. So innocent.

How do I approach this now? I throw my figurative dreams of being 'Dad of the Year' out the window, and sit next to her on the couch, trying to gather my thoughts.

"What's your favorite food?" I ask as she sits up straight and gives me her full attention. I love that we can talk like this, and that she's open to it all the time.

"Meatloaf," she says without thinking.

Again, there's my girl. Forsaking the norms of pizza or burgers.

"Okay," I say, nodding, trying to conjure the right lesson in my head. I don't know if I can work with meatloaf. "Can you imagine that there are people who *hate* meatloaf?"

Her serious face is confused for a moment, and she shrugs. "Well, they're wrong. Meatloaf is the best."

I stifle a laugh.

Okay, maybe meatloaf isn't the ticket to salvation here.

"What about Pepsi, you like that, right?"

"Yeah..."

"Well, I like Dr. Pepper. Some people prefer Coca-Cola. Or root beer. Or orange soda. Or none of them at all."

"Okay..." she shrugs again, and I don't think my point is coming across at all.

"Those sodas have been around for years. Even way before your great-grandfather, Pops, was born. Do you think they'd still be around now if people didn't like them?"

She shakes her head thoughtfully but stays quiet.

"It's the same thing with people, kiddo. Someone you think is 'cute' may not be cute to someone else. Everyone likes different things. Do you get what I'm saying?" God, I hope this is making fucking sense. I'm losing my way in my own head now.

"I get it." Her voice is soft as she leans onto my shoulder, sliding her arm through mine to hug tightly. "But does that mean that I'm wrong?"

Great. Now I've gone and made her feel like shit about herself and her opinions. *Way to go Dad.*

"No, no," I soothe, ruffling her hair. "It just means that everyone has opinions and feelings. There are lots of people that would agree with you, but there are also lots of people that wouldn't. Everybody is different. And everyone has a right to their own opinions and feelings. It's how you share them with the world that matters."

"So, if your new bass player is ugly, I shouldn't say anything."

That makes me laugh, and I can't help it. If that's what she got out of my stupid example, I guess it's good enough for now. I didn't mean for this to be a lecture, or 'teaching moment.'

"No. Please don't tell the bass player they're ugly."

"Can we watch Frozen now?"

Her question throws me way off since my brain is

still stuck on the soda metaphor, but I should be used to her sudden shifts in attention. Not that Charlie is flighty, but the focus of her intensity moves targets frequently.

"Sure…" I say, unravelling from her grip and grabbing the TV remote. Movies have become our love language. Especially Disney movies. We do our own version of Mystery Science Theater 2000 as we watch; critiquing everything from the dialogue to the animation. It's become a favorite pastime of ours, and somehow, we still find new things to comment on.

"Some people are worth melting for," Charlie says wistfully, quoting the snowman Olaf from the movie as she curls up next to me.

As I start the movie, I suddenly get the feeling we're heading into dangerous waters of her girlhood, and a fear starts to press its way down my spine. Cute bass players? Someone worth melting for?

Oh no…

My thoughts get interrupted by my phone blowing up with calls. It's my stressed manager Ian, no doubt freaking about our bassist problem again.

If we can't get a solid player locked in soon, our upcoming gigs are screwed. These days bands live and die by their streaming numbers. Tanking some shows means our fan loyalty takes a hit. I can't let everything we've built go down the drain.

"Dad, no," Charlie whines, bummed our movie night keeps getting messed with. I hate shutting off her protests, but this band crisis isn't going to solve itself.

I should answer.

I squeeze Charlie's shoulder, feeling guilty. I'm damned if I do, and damned if I don't. I know I need to fight this battle with the label not just for my creative pride, but to protect the career that will support her dreams someday too. As she smiles and snuggles in closer, I reluctantly turn my phone off, making a silent promise to myself that we'll get through this storm.

Somehow

Just not right this second.

four
this town

Tess

T he first day at a new job is always nerve wracking. My usual home turf involves high rise corner offices, stylish business suits, and triple-shot lattes. Now, I'm contending with grumbling trucks, thrift store jeans, and gas station coffee as I pull up to the gritty, low-profile warehouse space that houses Chaos Fuel's rehearsal studio.

The paint-peeled metal door groans loudly announcing my entrance. This is definitely out of my element, but I straighten my spine. The first rule of PR: Never let them see you sweat.

I pause, scanning the space, wary of interrupting the easy creative synergy of this band that might be happening, and I'm supposed to somehow harness. What do I really know about the alchemy behind inspiration in sessions like this? The closest my career has ever steered to actual music-making lately is damage control for drunken award show antics. This is totally new.

Seeing this unguarded creative habitat in action stirs an unease I can't quite place. These musicians live in a carefree, uninhibited headspace foreign from the calculated corporate waters I've sailed thus far. Witnessing the messy vitality of their collaborative sparks firsthand may demolish my long-held assumptions on rockstar personalities. Everything rides on my ability to adapt and realign perspectives, but maybe they'll just see me as an outsider incapable of ever capturing their true selves?

Imposter Syndrome creeps in despite my efforts. I'm used to commanding rooms, but this arena makes me question what value I can possibly contribute...or if I even speak the right language.

Taking a deep breath and straightening my shoulders, I dive in. My heels click conspicuously on the cracked cement floor, drawing the attention of the ragtag group clustered around a makeshift stage of amps and equipment.

Here we go.

"Who the hell's this?" grunts a shorter, stocky guy with dark hair clutching drumsticks, an unlit cigarette hanging from his lips. Emmett Cavenaugh. Chaos Fuel's trickster drummer. I'll need to be wary of him if the stories I've seen are correct.

My gaze darts around trying to mentally map territory critical to maneuvering this intro. The beat-up leather couch and mini fridge stocked with water bottles imply the lounge area. A cluster of mismatched chairs surround various sound equipment are likely the mockup control room hub. My eyes catch on scuffed up isolation booths for recording takes, duct tape barely holding acoustic foam panels onto worn wooden dividers.

I inch subtly closer, avoiding wires all over making precarious trails I'm certain to trip over if I have to walk anywhere. Nothing about this workspace conforms easily to every efficient, ergonomic, corporate office layout I've occupied for years. The fish-out-of-water sensation that started before I walked in, hits with full force now.

Before I can start into my carefully rehearsed introduction, one of the tall, handsome men steps forward smiling with a hand extended.

"You must be Tess! I'm Ian, the band manager." His British accent is adorable. Maybe I could love this job...

His friendly handshake steadies my nerves slightly. From the wary glances, I can already tell the suits versus creatives culture clash will be steep. But maybe Ian will prove to be an allied interpreter straddling both worlds. I know he used to be in a band himself. That could come in handy as we move forward.

Drawing a centering breath, I brace to convince these dubious rockstars that order and image can align with artistry.

"Daddy, come look at what me and June made," a little girl with long red curls calls from the corner, where three of them are huddled. My thoughts are instantly interrupted and derailed.

"In a minute, honey," says the most attractive man out of the bunch. The infamous Brad Chambers. His long blonde hair is perfectly messy, his strong jawline a mix between scruff and beard, his dark eyes are wary and guarded. The tattoos on his arms seem to dance when he moves. And it's all sexy as hell.

He's around the same age as me, early thirties, but he seems older and younger at the same time. He's definitely lived. I can't seem to keep my eyes off him. It's as if the rest of the room disappeared when our gazes met, and we're the only people in the room.

"I'm Brad Chambers," he says, stepping closer and shaking my hand. He seems reluctant or resigned. I can't tell which. But when his hand touches mine, it's warm, and an odd sensation flutters over my skin as if it's waking up from a long, dormant sleep. It's odd, and I resist the urge to shudder visibly when I let go.

"Nice to meet you," I finally say, pulling my shit together.

I stifle a surprised laugh as the compact drummer launches into an eccentric introduction.

"I'm Emmett Cavenaugh. Resident skin-smasher and all-around chaos conductor for this operation," he proclaims, giving an exaggerated bow. "When I'm not cracking the whip on these knuckleheads, you can find me trolling paranormal message boards for my podcast. Gotta chase those ghosts, baby."

I lift an eyebrow, uncertain if he's kidding but amused, nonetheless. Before I can inquire further, the lanky guitarist ambles up, nonchalantly blowing an unruly strand of Nordic blonde hair from his eyes.

"Name's Stefan Karlsson. Self-proclaimed legend," he offers a dramatic wink, relinquishing his cigarette to shake my hand loosely. "Watch your step around here though, I tend to leave trails of guitar picks everywhere I go. They breed in my pockets I think."

As he wanders off absently humming an intricate riff, I feel all the leftover tension begin to ease by their silly antics. Apparently, moods shift as quickly as the chords around here. But maybe these guys have more harmless depths than their prickly press implies.

"So," Ian says, clapping his hands together after an awkward silence covers us. "What do you need from us to get the good PR train rolling?"

Suddenly, I'm on the spot. I've prepared for this. I had it all planned out in my head before I walked in here, but it all flew out of my brain when Brad shook my stupid hand.

I'm a professional. I've been doing this for years. I've run my own teams, and suddenly, I'm reduced to that of a dumb schoolgirl in the presence of a crush. Not a brain cell to be found in my empty head.

Snap out of it, Tess.

"Well, to be honest, I'm just here to observe for the first few days," I say, grabbing at tethers of thought from the ether in my head. I think that was my plan. "I'd like to get a sense of the band before forming any solid strategies." At least it sounds like a reasonable thing to do. I'm pretty sure it's close to what I prepared. I do like to get a feel for things before diving in.

"Okay, that sounds good," Ian says, glancing at the band for any other input. None is forthcoming. They're all still eyeing me warily.

I'm the enemy. I get it. Loud and clear.

"You can sit with me over there," he points to the group of chairs alongside a tattered couch. "Our first auditioner should be here soon. We're just warming up."

"Sounds good," I mutter, following him to sit down. I make sure to avoid catching Brad's eye as I go. I get the feeling that's dangerous water to swim in.

But as I think that, I see him go over to the corner where three girls are huddled together over some project. He affectionately ruffles the redhead's hair as he leans over to inspect whatever it is they're working on. That must be Charlotte, his daughter. There's not much online about her or their relationship, but it's obvious from just their body language that there's something special in their bond.

My preconceptions about Brad Chambers, the magnetic frontman known for bedding groupies and trashing hotel rooms in years past, might be all wrong. Maybe there's more to him than that. Actually, seeing him now with his daughter, I'm sure there is.

One key thing about good public relations is that it isn't a mask, or a one-dimensional thing. The most important part is to tap into something relatable. Something everyone, or at least your target audience, can identify with. You need to show the world that you're human. Complex. Layered.

Like them.

I think I may have just uncovered Chaos Fuel's redemption.

Charlotte.

five
love no more

Brad

"**D**ad, check out this crazy creation we made!" Charlie waves me over to inspect the explosion of glue, fabric and glitter she orchestrated with the girls. I can't help grinning, mussing her vibrant red curls. No matter the chaos swirling round, her energetic spirit always lifts me up.

"That's awesome, kiddo. What is that? A guitar?" It looks like it might be a guitar. It's hard to tell with all the freaking glitter.

"It's a bass guitar," Ian's daughter Hayley announces proudly, taking the piece from her sister June to show me. "For the new person, to welcome them."

I arch a brow, impressed that they're being so thoughtful. I never in a million years would have thought to get a new band member a welcome present. But then, I'm mostly an asshole.

"Well, that's really cool," I say, grinning at her.

My smile fades a bit though, glancing toward Tess

standing rigid in her jeans and blouse while clutching her leather covered tablet. Not a strand of straight blonde hair out of place. She almost looks kind of silly playing corporate doll in our grungy studio. I don't know. Having a label rep hovering around us rubs me wrong, even if she is here to polish our reputation.

Ian trails off his conversation with her seeing most of us aren't exactly welcoming Tess with open arms. An awkward silence descends on the room until Emmett shatters it by tapping his drum sticks wildly. "Who's ready to audition our next victim?" He grins deviously in Tess's direction.

Subtle as always.

I shoot an agitated glance toward Tess, resenting her upcoming critique of our creative process. Her pursed lips take scribbled notes on her tablet tracking the day like some clinical fucking science experiment. I can't shake an uneasy feeling about everything riding on nailing this bassist search without it changing the raw vibe Chaos Fuel's built on. We have to find somebody soon, but we also have to be picky about who we let in.

We've been doing this a long fucking time. As long as Charlie's been alive, in fact. And we're finally getting where we wanted to go all along. We're signed with a label. People know who the fuck we are. But with it comes complications. Like bad press, and crazy social media. When we first started together, things like that didn't matter. The music did.

And now? Now we have a 'handler' to manage our

'image.' We're getting choked by greedy corporate fingers not even polite enough to thank us after they fuck us.

Tess hanging around now to *observe* is getting to me. It's like we're a fucking zoo exhibit or some shit. Caged animals on display for entertainment. But only if we entertain in the *right* way. Only if we put a certain foot forward.

Only if...

My thoughts get interrupted as the door to the practice space creaks open, and our first 'victim' as Emmett called them, walks in. I hand the artwork back to the girls and take a deep breath, steeling myself for the long day ahead.

My fingers rake restlessly through my hair, its overgrown length starting to feel like a noose cinching my restless thoughts too tight. I shift my weight between my feet as our first prospect enters, temptation to bolt itching at me.

Fucking label leashes.

We've been through this before. Many times. Too many times. And it's never fun. Now it's worse with judging eyes on us. It's almost as though we're on that stupid TV talent show that Indigo King is in London for, even though we're not the ones trying out.

I'm a frontman. The spotlight is always on me. I'm used to it to a point. This is different somehow. I don't feel like I'm the one in control here, and the strings puppeting me are now visible with Tess right in front of us. And as those ropes tighten, my grip on the steering wheel of my life slides ominously.

I don't like where this is headed.

As we play, Tess circles, watching us like some freak show and irritation simmers beneath the surface at her intrusion. Yet some buried part of me prickles awake too each time our gazes catch.

She moves through the ragged studio completely oblivious to how those curve-hugging jeans hold my distracted eyes. How the way she bites her bottom lip when she concentrates makes my blood sing. I grit my teeth, tamping down the reckless thoughts her unintended temptation sparks inside of me.

As we take a break between auditions, I peel off towards the fridge for a water bottle. Out of nowhere, Tess appears on the same trajectory, nearly colliding into my side. I reach out reflexively, hands catching just above her hips to gently steady her on her feet.

"Oh gosh, sorry about that!" Tess jumps slightly at the contact, cheeks flushing as she adjusts the tablet clasped to her chest.

"No problem," I murmur. But I don't immediately release my light grip, that subtle floral scent of hers clouding my senses. Hazel eyes lift to mine for a hovering moment, something uncertain flickering in their depths before skittering away.

I drop my hands awkwardly, taking a subtle step back out of her personal space. Tess tucks a loose wisp of golden hair behind her ear, lips curving into a tentative smile.

"Well, uh...excuse me," she gestures politely towards

the water stash before scooting around me. The absence of her warmth pulls at me unexpectedly.

What the fuck?

I run a hand roughly through my hair again, exhaling frustration I can't place. *Get it together, man.* Maybe I need some air to clear my head.

The last thing we need complicating this bassist hunt is me mixing business with pleasure, no matter how fine the suit. *I've got to keep clear focus without unnecessary distractions*, I remind myself firmly. Even intriguing distractions who seem to read into every obvious stare no matter how quickly I flick my restless glance away.

Something in her eyes, the way she studies me, makes me think she can see past the frontman façade that I put on, and it's making me uncomfortable.

Vulnerable.

I don't fucking do vulnerable.

six
hanging by a
moment

Tess

I stare sightlessly at the cursor blinking impatiently for input, my new band homepage draft mockingly blank. A chaotic maze of noise filters in from the band goofing off across the studio space yet again. I massage my temples, stuffing down irritation.

Focus, Tess.

I became a sought-after crisis handler by cultivating a smooth, unflappable armor in the face of chaos. Meltdowns, scandals, disasters - bring it on. But something about this ragtag crew gets under my skin and throws me off-center. Makes me feel exposed. Vulnerable.

It's too familiar...echoes of messy rooms strewn with empty bottles; broken promises slurred angrily through the wall vents. The only escape I had was a fierce work ethic to bury those memories under my polished accomplishments. Until my ambition felt less like atonement and more like armor.

I rose above it all eventually. So why does this makeshift studio dredge up ghosts I outran long ago?

These guys don't resemble the instability of my past. Not entirely. They just create freely, heedlessly, chasing inspiration wherever she might lead that day. No wonder the suits at the label struggle to harness such explosive creative forces.

I shake off the memories clawing at my composure. This project matters. I need to guide these passionate visionaries toward the wider acclaim they deserve. My pulse rises, rallying my focus. I can see that their magic is worth fighting for. I only hope they'll let me help instead of viewing me as the enemy. So far, I'm not doing so great at that part.

Navigating the makeshift craft services table thrown together with nearby take-out for our lunch, I cautiously retrieve a bottled tea, wary of interrupting the band's camaraderie permeating the space. Their laughter and inside banter form an exclusive barrier no corporate outsider could possibly break through. Not even me. And I don't consider myself to be 'corporate.'

I find myself hovering uncertainly along the periphery, seeking any conversational opening to bridge this isolating divide. But most chatter dies abruptly if I stray too close; if I say anything.

Emmett grunts dismissively through a mouthful of sub sandwich while Stefan seems suddenly engrossed inventorying his guitar case minutiae.

Only Brad holds my gaze steady for a piercing moment. That magnetic tug sparks against my will once more. Flustered, I drop my eyes and retreat closer to Ian's more welcoming orbit, taking the chair next to him and his daughters. However, the ghost sensation of Brad's studying me lingers - equal parts searing and comforting.

I wonder briefly, dangerously, what sharing their world more intimately might reveal about the intriguing contradiction that smolders beneath his brooding, bad boy façade. There's more there, and I want to know what it is.

I push aside that reckless thought, rallying my focus toward thawing the band's relations professionally before tapping into anything personal. They need to see that I'm on their side. I'm not the enemy here, even though I work for the label.

"So, out of the three so far, are there any standouts for you guys?" I ask, trying to break yet another awkward silence.

"I liked the last one. *Toby*," Charlie swoons. "He was super cute."

Hayley and June giggle in agreement, hiding their smiles behind their hands as they blush. They're about Charlies age, maybe a little younger, and all three girls are adorable.

Brad rolls his eyes at his daughter with a dramatic sigh. "We talked about this..."

They talked about cute guys? Now that's a conversation I would have liked to have been in on.

Charlie swings her feet, her bright pink Converse sneakers sway as she talks. "I know. But he *was* cute. I can't help it."

"I thought I was the cute one," Emmett protests, pretending to be offended. He holds his hand to his chest, mortally wounded. "You're breaking my heart here."

She waves a dismissive hand at him with the confidence only an eight-year-old girl can muster while breaking someone's heart. "You're still cute, but Toby was *super cute*. His smile was just..." she drifts off with a dreamy sigh.

Brad glances at me, as if looking for my reaction, and I'm not sure if he's checking that I agree that Toby was cute, or my response to his daughter's antics. I just smile and shrug. It's vague enough to cover both scenarios.

Not going to lie, Toby was hot, but I don't think his personality meshed with the band's. He was a bit too flashy, and that's Brad's job. I could see that Brad wasn't too impressed by him either.

"That's my girl," Brad sighs, tugging on a lock of Charlie's hair. "The Disney Princess in love with love, but who would probably turn her prince into a frog."

She sighs again with a dramatic eye roll. "*Only* if he deserved it."

Watching the two of them interact is heart-warming. It's as if I'm getting an inside glimpse into the side of Brad that no one has seen before. The easy banter between them makes me wish I'd had that kind of relationship when I was her age – not the constant battles I had to be a part of. They have a unique connection.

It's special.

A settling hush covers the practice space as lunch winds down. Chatter stops amidst the clinking mismatched dishes being cleared. Soon everyone's creative endeavors resume in separate pockets - Charlie is engrossed guiding her friends in some sparkly masterpiece as Ian supervises, the other guys step out to have a smoke, leaving only Brad and I lingering uncertainly.

I debate different conversation openers I could use to chip away at the obvious hostilities between us when Brad unexpectedly breaks the strained silence.

"So, what deep analysis are you cooking up to fix us wayward rockers on that tablet of yours?" His wry tone echoes the band's arm's length weariness towards my purpose here.

I smile softly, sensing an opening. "Honestly? Witnessing you all so in sync jamming today...I don't know that you actually need fixing."

Brad's stoic features flicker with surprise at this praise-adjacent observation. I continue gently, "Don't get me wrong, image tweaks would definitely help. But tampering with your core musical dynamic could devastate everything special between you all. That's not my aim here."

He studies me intently, perhaps glimpsing for the first time the potential fan glimmering beneath my cool handler exterior. Something in his expression shifts. It's still guarded, but a notch less combative.

We might find common ground yet.

"So, what is your aim? Exactly?" he asks, and I swear it's real curiosity. His interest in my being here has finally piqued beyond simple resentment.

"Well, current public opinion is that you guys are spoiled brats who only care about partying." I may as well be honest with him.

He doesn't seem surprised, and his lips twitch into a wry smile. "Spoiled brats, huh?"

"Their words. Not mine," I clarify. "At least, that's *Blindsided's* take on things."

"Oh, good old *Blindsided*," he sighs, looking skyward as he rubs at the stubble on his chin. "The holy gospel according to pretentious assholes."

He's not wrong. *Blindsided* is known to walk on the wrong side of journalistic integrity. They have no problem publishing whatever they think will grab readers' attention, even if it's untrue. I've had to deal with them before in my line of work, but there's no negotiating with assholes bent on making a splash. They like to hide behind 'anonymous sources' for their alleged 'fact finding.' They take the tiniest seed of truth and warp the hell out of it for a headline.

"Agreed. But unfortunately, people do believe everything they read." I glance up at him, realizing how much taller he is than me. I am not small by any stretch of the imagination, but next to him I'm feeling downright petite. My senses are starting to overload standing so close to him like this, so I take a small step sideways to give myself some breathing room.

Being close to Brad Chambers does something to me.

Something I've not experienced before, and I can't put a name to it because I can't completely describe it. I feel... *weird*. Strange. Disoriented. It's as if my sensibility has taken a fucking hike. It's got to be his rockstar persona, blinding me to reality.

I'm dumbstruck. And I don't like it.

"Do you think our fans read that bullshit and believe it?" he asks, snapping me out of my stupor.

"That's hard to gauge directly," I admit, pulling myself back into the conversation. More like dragging myself back. "According to Eliza, sales are down, which is either a coincidence, or a direct correlation. We have no real way of knowing. So, I'm here to try to turn that around, regardless of the cause."

"But if it's not the cause..." He's guarded again. The carefully disguised shields are rising again.

Damnit.

"If it's not the cause, a little positive PR can't hurt, right?" I ask, hoping to make my case that I'm not the bad guy. "I really am here to help. Not turn you into something you're not. I swear."

"But what do you think? What's your *professional* opinion?"

I try not to bristle at the way he asks the question. He's starting to get defensive, but I need to keep being honest with him if this is going to work.

"I belong to a few Chaos Fuel fan forums under a pseudonym for research. Your loyal fans stand by you guys. Though some do complain you seem...distant lately in meet-and-greets and interviews. Not fully present."

Brad's stoic expression grows thoughtful as he digests this, but he doesn't say anything. I continue gently, "I won't pretend to grasp the pressures you guys deal with. But those ride-or-die fans just want to feel heard beyond the rock God façade, you know? Feel *seen*."

I hold my breath awaiting his reaction at me quoting directly from forum messages. Brad watches me curiously. "So, you're embedded with our fans' chatter? Why not just ask the label for data?"

I exhale, smiling softly. "Numbers are easy to collect from socials. Nuance is harder. I prefer to go to the source if I can."

Something about this transparency seems to resonate. Brad's expression shifts subtly from wary to intrigue. "Guess you're more than just a suit, *Handler Tess...*"

I flush, strangely pleased by his acknowledgment I've done my homework here. It's a small win, but my heartbeat quickens triumphantly all the same.

He studies me closer, and I do my best to keep my own guard down. Show him that I'm being honest with him. I think it works because something manifests in his dark gray eyes; an acceptance of some kind that I pray means he won't fight this like I know he's wanted to all along.

"Okay," he says with a slow nod as he shoves his hands into the back pockets of his jeans. His long hair sways with the movement. My fingers start to itch to want to reach out and see what it feels like, the shiny strands are tempting. "So long as you're not looking to change anything. Maybe show different sides of us or something, but don't try to make us into something we're not."

I shake my head determinedly. "Absolutely. I would never try to change you guys. That's not what I do at all. You have my word on that."

His features smooth with relief and his shoulders relax a little. It's as if I've put out a fire, or eased his mind somehow, and it alleviates something inside of me too. We understand each other now, or at least, he understands me. I still have to figure out the enigma that is Brad Chambers.

There are layers to him that contradict each other so diametrically, that it's hard to compute. Like how loving and affectionate he is with his daughter, versus how aloof and detached he appears in the press. Like I told him, even with fans he stands out as separate, like he's holding his true self hidden away.

He needs to let the real Brad Chambers out for all to see. I'm starting to see it. And I like it.

I like it a lot.

Maybe too much.

seven
down

Brad

"Well, I say we just grab that one hippie dude with the van painted like the Mystery Machine as our bassist and call it a day," Emmett proclaims, twirling a drumstick irreverently.

A round of groans from the rest of us echoes as we lounge about debriefing on the day's marathon of bassist auditions. My fingers knead my forehead vainly hoping to massage away the tension headache brewing there all afternoon.

"What? Dude was decent enough and brings that carefree vibe, ya know?" Emmett continues, undeterred. I can't tell if he's kidding or not. I really hope he's not being serious.

Stefan flicks a bottle cap at Emmett's head in reply. "Cause Scooby-Doo truly captures the chaotic essence of our sound."

Their bickering fades to background noise as I notice

Tess camping beside Charlie's craft corner. She's smiling ear-to-ear at some critter taking shape under my daughter's guidance. I can't lie, my hang-ups over Tess's involvement are easing a little seeing how effortlessly she bonds with Charlie.

This bassist search pressure feels less crushing watching their giggling exchange. Tess playfully dots a glue-dripping rhinestone nose on Charlie's creature. Seeing her laugh it up freely with Charlie kicks my protectiveness into overdrive. I rarely let random women buddy up to my girl. Not after my past girlfriends forced me to break things off, devastating Charlie. She grows attached quickly. Too quickly. Watching tears stain my little girl's pillow as the harsh reality of it all dawned on her still shreds my heart. I swore not to blink at another dazzling smile until I was sure about the longevity of the relationship. And that's hard to come by in this fucking industry. Especially when all everyone wants is a piece of me. A piece of the limelight.

Their craft corner laughter keeps pulling my gaze back. Tess admires some fluffy feathered thing Charlie made, both grinning ear to ear. My pulse revs up. Charlie latches on quickly to positive feedback. She'll be bummed when Tess likely moves on. Still, I can't deny that seeing my baby girl light up with simple joy always tugs at my heart too.

"Check out those incredible lashes, sparkling diva style! No mythical creature could out-dazzle this." Tess winks conspiratorially, adding more glitter. Charlie absolutely beams under the spotlight of her attention.

Noticing my reluctant staring, Tess glances up. The openness shining from her sucker punches my knee-jerk misgivings. For just a second, stripped from image or agenda, she's purely present with my daughter. And it floods over me like a tidal wave.

Ian clears his throat, drawing all of our wandering attention back again. "Alright lads, and ladies," he amends, nodding graciously towards Tess, "Let's keep spirits high, yeah? Bassists with chemistry for our dynamic obviously aren't as numerous as we'd hoped, but hidden gems remain out there. We've still got a few days to go. People still to see."

"Ugh, I'll pass on more duds like that arrogant prick who bragged about finishing bass school 'with honors,'" Emmett jeers, using exaggerated air quotes before mimicking playing an overzealous riff.

"We could post flyers at every Guitar Center branch as a last resort. That's still a thing, right?" Stefan suggests half-heartedly with a wry chuckle before glancing Tess's way. "Maybe your PR master brain there has a better idea?"

I follow his gaze to Tess, feeling an odd defensiveness about Stefan's mildly skeptical tone directed her way after witnessing her bonding with Charlie.

"Who? Me? Oh gosh, no pressure on me for audition solutions," Tess laughs graciously, obviously nervous to be put on the spot like this. "Though if fan enthusiasm matters, perhaps floating wildcard chances to the public to engage them might instill some sort of community goodwill?"

"What do you mean?" I ask. "Open auditions to fans?"

She shrugs, but I can see the doubt now cloud her features, and I feel guilty that my tone was as skeptical as Stefan's was.

"Sure. Why not?" Her chin juts out slightly, defiant, and stubborn. "Who's to say where you'll find someone who fits? Everyone you've seen today, or will see in the coming days, you already know. Maybe you need to start looking elsewhere?"

Ian beams supportively. "See lads, fresh perspectives, open minds, the stuff dreams are made of. It wouldn't hurt to put out some feelers to the fanbase, right?"

I follow his enthusiasm with an uncertain glance toward Stefan and Emmett to gauge their reception. It's always hard to predict which outlandish ideas might ignite their spark.

Stefan offers a cautious thumbs up. "Worth a shot if our well is running dry with the same old professional prospects."

Emmett practically vibrates with excitement. "Dude, this is literally my whole jam. Let's give all garage legends-in-waiting a chance to bring the noise."

I should have expected Emmett to embrace stirring up chaos. He lives to shatter any monotony he comes across in the world, and not in the most constructive way.

Memories of the last media circus we inadvertently spawned fill my mind. We had a guest bass guitarist from

Murderous Crows sit in on our set at a festival when our last bassist literally ran away, and the thought of it feeds my unease. We gained some notoriety from that stunt once the reasons got out – namely Emmett's stupid pranks. I don't think it did us any favors.

Hopefully Tess truly comprehends the fallout potential going off script like this invites when dealing directly with fans. We could end up alienating people in the long run. Then again, welcoming a little mayhem sometimes breeds magic.

I don't have a lot of choice here. Even if I wanted to go against everyone, which I'm not sure I do, I'd be outnumbered.

"Great," I mutter under my breath. "Let's ask the fans."

The pungent aroma of burgers sizzling on the grill surrounds us in the vinyl-laden diner booth. I sink back comfortably, eying the flurry of Chaos Fuel hashtags and graphics splashed across the screen as Tess works busily storyboarding Instagram posts.

Charlie leans over, curiously munching fries, captivated by Tess's swift creative powers manifesting before our very eyes. Even I'm cautiously intrigued with what she'll come up with to lure potential bass hopefuls from the virtual woodwork.

"We obviously want to spotlight the fun perks of

joining a chart-topping act without overhyping in an overly commercial or off-putting way," Tess narrates briskly, fingers flying across tablet commandingly.

"Ooh, you should use that picture of Stefan trying on that fan's big sunglasses from the meet-and-greet last month," Charlie suggests brightly through a mouthful of cheeseburger. "That was hilarious. I'd want to join that band."

Amused pride swells in my chest seeing Charlie intuitively understand hooking an audience while this behind-the-scenes glimpse of image strategy unfolds. I guess a music legacy of some kind was inevitable, given that both me and her stepfather are musicians, but her keen marketing instincts still amaze me.

"Look out Handler Tess," I grin. "Someone might be gunning for your job." I nudge Charlie with my forearm playfully.

"She's a total natural," Tess smiles, and her gaze lifts, meeting mine. Something in her expression shifts subtly. Lingering sparks glitter mischievously between us. "You Chambers' have a formidable talent of drawing people in..."

Tess nibbles her bottom lip, on the verge of saying more it seems. But hesitation flashes briefly across her features. Is Tess flirting? Before I can reorient my scrambled thoughts, she ducks behind her tablet, tapping purposefully.

"Let's stay focused. We need to finish brainstorming this audition call-out, okay?" Tess tosses casually over her shoulder.

But a telling flush grazes her neck contradicting that cool recovery attempt. My pulse inexplicably skips. Was that loaded compliment aimed my way? Or is hope clouding my judgment?

Am I hopeful?

eight
turn

Tess

"**D**uuuuude! Get over here, you gotta see this cat shredding in a cheetah costume."

Emmett's raucous laughter echoes through the studio space. We're gathered around various screens critiquing the influx of video auditions generated in the last few days since our Instagram post went unexpectedly viral.

I hover at Emmett's shoulder, squinting critically at the pixelated fur-clad bassist currently giving an impassioned performance. Was embracing the band's 'chaos' brand intentional or mere social media happenstance? It's hard to tell. Either way, it's a hard pass.

My eyes wander, seeking Brad's, but he's engrossed across the room strumming along expressively to a muscular girl absolutely owning the intricate bass rhythms she's playing. Then she goes hands-free and it's clear she wasn't really playing after all.

A strange pang passes through me witnessing his

absorption there despite the outcome. Is it jealousy? What the hell would I be jealous about?

We connected at dinner the other night. All three of us did. And it's been all I can think about since. Brad and I both seemed to let down our guard for a little while, and Charlie was the catalyst. She has somehow needled her way into my heart in the time it took for one freaking meal. One freaking day. Hell, they both have, if I'm being honest. And I don't know what to do with that. It's clearly throwing me off my professional game, and that's something that never happens. But then, I don't usually immerse myself with clients' lives like this.

I tamp it all down, redirecting back to the task at hand: filtering online standouts to potentially call back live. But my focus wavers again when another howl of amusement bursts out from Stefan at some new outrageous submission.

I rub my eyes, echoes of raucous video riffs grating on my last nerve. I can't believe no one's taking this seriously. A call goes out begging for fans' help, and we get flooded with head-scratching stunt audition clips. I thought maybe we'd uncover some hidden talents. But all I'm seeing are posts for shock value and nothing more.

My heart sinks.

Even Ian can't redirect focus back to finding suitable prospects amid all the pageantry on display. Obviously that one girl captivated Brad more than her actual potential to mesh with the real band.

My frustration simmers longer as Emmett keeps fanning the chaos flames for giggles. My leg starts to jitter impatiently. It feels like placing our PR fate in fans' hands has epically backfired if no one respects the opportunity it really is. I stupidly ignored the variable of risking legitimacy just for visibility.

Brad meets my eyes, clocking my vibe shift. But another jaw-dropping clip draws his attention before we connect. Creeping doubts dig into my psyche. This is a nightmare. A fucking nightmare. And it's all my fault. This is all going to boomerang and bite me in the ass.

Some expert I am.

"Dad, go back!" Charlie suddenly urges, tugging Brad's shirt. "That guy with the beanie was way cuter than that surfer dude."

Brad's eyes flare incredulously. "Pretty sure musical chemistry and talent is the goal here. Not dreamy crushes, baby girl. He probably can't play."

But his protest gets overridden by her persistence. Sighing, Brad scrolls socials backtracking to some long-haired bassist. I drift over and peer closer despite myself. I cross my fingers, hoping for a miraculous savior to appear on the screen.

Shaggy ink-black strands peek from a knit beanie as soulful hazel eyes glint mischievously at the camera. The frame shakes following his fluid movements around the room, but tight low-end runs punctuate a solid solo.

My critical mind perks up. His technical skills are meeting up with a distinctive style. Glancing around, the rest of the band have mirrored expressions of pleasant surprise. Maybe method exists in this madness after all.

"Not bad..." Emmett concedes. "Not bad at all."

We all crowd around the laptop as Brad starts the video over from the beginning. It's as if we're all holding our collective breath that this isn't a mirage, or some AI contrived joke of some kind.

When the video ends, the guys all look at each other, but don't say a word. Ian is the first to voice a real opinion, and being a former bass player himself before a hand injury, I value his take.

"You have to admit, the guy's got chops," he shrugs. "Some of those progressions...I couldn't do that even in my prime."

Silence falls again as everyone considers what Ian's said. A lot is riding on this, and I think the novelty of the crank videos has finally worn off.

This is important.

Charlie glances around, her brows knit in confusion. "Is he the one Daddy? Did I find you a bass player, even though he's cute?"

With an arched eyebrow, and perhaps even a little mirth, he strokes her hair gently. "We'll have to see, but I think you did, baby girl. I think you did."

She beams as she bounces on her toes, Hayley and June joining in on her celebration as they start jumping around us, giggling, and laughing.

Brad drags his eyes from his daughter to look at Ian and me. "Let's find this guy, and bring him in. See if he's for real."

"Hell yeah," Emmett chimes in. "Shit's getting real now."

"Shit's been real for a while now," Stefan says, his face unreadable as he walks away. "Welcome to the show."

The rollercoaster of emotions from the last five minutes makes my head hurt. From Charlie and the girls' excitement to Brad's reticence, Emmett's awakening, and now Stefan's odd reaction, I'm not sure what to make of any of it.

Part of me is relieved we might have a real prospect on our hands thanks to my idea. But another part of me is wary that it might still go wrong. And then there's the part that keeps glancing over at Brad to see if he's glancing at me, like some stupid high school crush, making me feel as immature as Charlie.

I knew coming in that this was going to be complicated. I'm in unknown territory. What I didn't expect was getting emotionally invested in any of it, or anyone. That's not what I do, or how I work. I keep a distance.

But now, I care.

Damnit.

nine
dissolve me

Brad

I lean against the cracked tile counter in my cramped kitchen, the faint smell of burnt coffee permeating the space. My eyes drift over the disorderly mess: a precarious tower of splattered mixing bowls, a dusting of cocoa powder, the dregs of our late movie night ice cream melted to sticky puddles across the table. Hints of Charlie everywhere, breathing new life into my sterile bachelor existence.

My gaze lands on Charlie's glitter glue sticking to the brown leather couch, stubborn sparkly remnants glinting back no matter how much I scrub. The mottled carpet still embedded with crumbs from impromptu floor picnics no vacuum can quite pull up. Mismatched throw pillows and blankets in bright colors she lovingly assembled into a cozy nest. Signs of vitality slicing through the dim, muted tones of my typically lone refuge.

It feels good.

I can't help grinning as I take in the comfortable mess

Charlie's made here - my boring bachelor pad is now bursting with color and energy only an eight-year-old tornado of a girl could bring. This cramped place hasn't felt much like home lately. It's just been somewhere to pass out after late shows and even later nights at the studio. But with Charlie's bubbly laughter filling up the empty space, it already feels warmer.

The grin deepens remembering Charlie ranting about messed up details as we watched movies last night. She takes analyzing that cartoon world so seriously, pointing out things that shatter believability for her eight-year-old brain. We made a game of finding plot holes and cheap animation cheats. Her frown would get deeper with each dramatic eyeroll until laughter finally exploded out at particularly stupid parts.

Watching her crack up like that clinches my throat sometimes. Because underneath the smarty pants act, those carefree little kid giggles poke out. Reminding me of the childhood she got cheated out of with me gone more than around. Each gig or schedule change erasing our plans probably dimmed that light in her a little over the years. Sure, Jude is there, but I'm her real fucking dad. I should have been there more.

If I don't screw this visit up, could moments like last night bring that spark back for real? Could six weeks heal old wounds and rebuild trust if I stick to my promises for once? I don't flake on purpose. Not anymore. But it still doesn't feel like enough. It'll never be enough to make up for lost time. Being here consistently matters more than even the fun stuff we get into. I know this.

I know this.

The stability in my crash pad these last few years probably looks monumental through a kid's eyes. Eyes that somehow still gaze at me with more patience than I deserve most days.

My smile falters though, thinking about how short-lived this visit is. Ren being gone these weeks meant Charlie and me wouldn't get our usual time together. Yet Charlie asked to stay with me instead of taking that over-seas trip. *That means something.* I know getting thrown into Dad duty full-time these couple months won't be easy. But I'm actually loving it.

Could I get used to having her lighting up my days like this all the time? Or even just more often? That question already ties my gut in knots. I need to keep doing better.

It's probably best I focus on the whirlwind already lined up for tomorrow when we meet that wildcard bass player from the internet. The one goofy video Charlie picked out that weirdly grabbed us. Was it just crazy luck with the whole internet call-out? Or maybe some deeper connection exists out there guiding strangers together somehow.

I like to believe in fate. That things happen for a reason. But does everything? Or only important things? Maybe just the small things?

Who the fuck knows.

My tornado of thoughts shifts unexpectedly to Tess. There's some magnetic pull happening there I wasn't expecting either. One that gets harder to ignore the more we talk. The image of her sweet smile, those blonde strands falling across her graceful neck as we chatted over dinner...keeps replaying in my brain like a song stuck on repeat.

I chuckle to myself remembering Tess huddled with Charlie in the studio space, both gluing rhinestones on some fluffy critter creation. Their giggling girl talk, and easy camaraderie stirred that fierce protectiveness in me as always. I can't help it after people have let my girl down before.

But something in the genuine warmth shining through in Tess's smile put me at ease. The way she gave Charlie her full attention instead of that distant distraction adults often slide into around kids. How thoughtful questions brought Charlie out of her initially shy shell little by little.

And those sly winks and whispers they exchanged like co-conspirators, pushed me over the edge. Tess didn't just humor Charlie's arts and crafts hobby. She somehow knew exactly which details would make it epic in a kid's eyes.

Seeing Charlie's beam widen as she bonds with someone new usually worries me. But watching Tess win her over inch-by-inch filled me with other emotions I can't quite name yet. Ones that quicken my pulse and clench my chest unexpectedly.

Maybe Tess understands the secrets of brightening a child's world better than most. She hasn't said anything specific about it, but I get the sense that her current position is hard won. She's a fighter. I recognize that weight in her even if the details of it stayed locked up tight.

My thoughts flash to the deflected questions whenever our conversations turn personal. Her slowed reactions those times emotions almost cracked the surface before she re-tightened her control. I recognize that hyper-vigilance of not letting anyone too close.

I saw it in mirrors for years when I could bring myself to even fucking look. Felt the weight of the baggage dragging behind each step, screaming, *don't look back*. Every new town, every new band, *just run*. Keep chaos always circling to outpace the demons nipping at my heels.

Maybe Tess had a rough upbringing too. Hard things that force you to grow up quick and affect you for a long time after. Like how I started putting up walls early so I wouldn't keep getting hurt anymore by people who were supposed to protect me. Those survival instincts kicking in teaching you not to feel too much or need anyone.

Could two people broken in similar jagged ways find an unexpected safe harbor in each other down the line? Past and future colliding, then realigning into something steadier together?

The thought doesn't scare me as much as it probably should. But not much scares me anymore.

Whatever she's survived, it clearly fine-tuned an empathy that reaches free spirits like Charlie. I ought to resent an outsider cracking those shields around my daughter. Yet with Tess, I can't summon the same wariness I normally would. And that might be what shakes me more than anything.

What is it about Tess that makes me willing to completely drop my guard for her? And why don't I feel like fighting it?

My leg bounces restlessly as I debate grabbing another beer or trying to force sleep. Charlie's light snores drift from her room down the hall, but my brain spins too fast to shut off. Before I overthink the impulse, I grab my phone to call Tess.

I stare at her name glowing in my contacts, finger hovering indecisively. *Come on, man. It's just a work call.* I hit dial before my nerve fails.

She answers on the third ring. "Brad?"

"Hey, sorry. I know it's late. This wildcard bass player thing has just been bugging me."

Smooth, Chambers. Real fucking subtle.

Tess laughs softly. "You and me both. It's unconventional but that video...he has something special, right? I can't get his sound out of my head."

I exhale, relieved she's as preoccupied, and by the musicality not just the uncertainty. Or the guy's alleged 'cuteness.'

"Exactly. Like his style is familiar but totally unique too?" I pace aimlessly, enthusiasm spilling out. "I don't know why I'm so obsessed about figuring this guy out all of a sudden."

A prickly silence follows my clumsy transparency. I squeeze my eyes shut cursing internally. *Way to play it cool, dumbass.* I scramble to recover some ground. "Uh, anyway, sorry to bug you after hours. I just value your take on this whole crazy thing."

Her soft breath fills the brief quiet until she speaks gently. "You're not bugging me at all. I'm glad you called." My stomach flips oddly. She continues, "This is uncharted territory for me too, remember? We'll figure things out together."

The sincerity in her words bands tight around my chest. I clear my throat roughly, fighting all the foreign feelings. "Right. Cool. So, what do we know about him? Any ideas of what to expect?"

I hear shuffling on Tess's end. "Ian's been handling the contact, but let's see, what little social media he has says his name's Dakota. No last name though."

"Hmm...Dakota." I roll the name around my head trying to conjure some solid mental image of tomorrow's guest. I know what the dude looks like, and how he plays, but absolutely nothing else. "Well that tells us exactly nothing."

Tess laughs, and the sound warms my chest. "Very mysterious. His technique seems mostly self-taught and adventurous. Lots of unexpected chord changes and rhythms."

"So, you really think he could work with our sound?" I switch the phone to my other ear, curiosity spiking.

"Absolutely. That raw creative energy could be exactly what you guys need." Tess pauses, tone thoughtful. "The passion reminds me of seeing you all perform actually."

I freeze, my heart racing strangely at her praise. I clear my throat, fishing for composure. "What, you saying I look passionate up there too?"

"I'd never feed that rockstar ego too much, but..." Tess's teasing voice trails off suggestively. Heat rushes into my neck and I snort out an awkward laugh to cover my flustered reaction. An odd tension creeps into the silence until Tess redirects. "Anyway, guess we'll find out more soon."

"Yeah, guess so." I hesitate, grasping for excuses to prolong this call. Longing to know more about what lurks beneath her polished exterior too. But I'm feeling awkward as fuck and can't think of a smooth line. "So... read any good books lately?"

Tess giggles at my random question. "Oh gosh, I wish I had time to read books. Between prepping for this new role and trying to have some semblance of a social life, free time is pretty scarce. My Netflix queue is embarrassing."

I smile, settling back into the couch and propping my feet up. "No judgment here. Unless we're talking reality shows. Please tell me you have better taste than that."

"Hey! Don't come at me for The Great British Bake Off," Tess protests playfully. "That show is a national treasure."

"If you say so." I chuckle. "But nah, I feel you on the no free time thing. Usually by the time I get Charlie to bed I just veg out to dumb videos too. Adulting is so glamorous, right?"

Tess hums in amused agreement. "Oh yeah, peak rockstar living over here. Yesterday's mascara is still clinging to dear life and remnants of mac and cheese dinners past are now stuck on my nice work blouses."

Her self-deprecating humor makes me grin. "Oh, come on, I bet you still look hot as hell covered in cheese dust." The flirtatious words slips out unintentionally. "Uh, I mean...you know, put together and stuff."

"Wow, don't overdo the compliments there, Casanova," Tess teases. I hear rustling like she's getting comfortable. "But seriously, I'm loving this glimpse behind the consummate rocker exterior. The great Brad Chambers does normal people things, who knew?"

I lean forward, letting her gentle ribbing thaw me further. "I mean, washing dishes and paying bills aren't quite as glamorous as trashing hotel rooms. But hot showers and homemade food make up for it."

Her answering laugh chimes melodically over the line. "No complaints about the hot showers I bet. Do rockstars still have groupies sneaking in hoping to share?"

My skin prickles at her flirty probing. Two can play this game. "Maybe back in the day. But word must've gotten out that I'm a total dud now. My wild days dried up once the wrinkles set in."

"I sincerely doubt that," Tess says, a smile lurking beneath the words. "You're certainly aging well from what I've seen..." The suggestive comment hangs invitingly.

I wet my lips, mouth suddenly dry. "Yeah well, settling down changes things. Most nights it's just me and Netflix these days too. Much to Charlie's annoyance when she's stuck with me. Though with her, we stick to Disney."

I hear sheets shift, and I try hard not to imagine Tess

curled up in bed. And fail. "Mm, no arguments here that snuggly movie nights sound better than partying too hard. Though I wouldn't say no to letting loose every so often."

I swallow thickly as tempting visuals flood my mind. I can actually feel the blood heating up in my veins.

Focus, Chambers...

I steer us to safer waters before my thoughts derail completely. "Yeah...so, uh, you got any hidden talents besides saving rockstar reputations?"

Tess hums thoughtfully across the line. The flirtatious tension cooks deliciously in each light probe and redirection.

I'd hoped for a connection like this but wasn't sure it would manifest. I didn't know if she'd be receptive.

Yet here we are. Just two people connecting via some random cell tower under the cloak of night.

This is fucking awesome.

ten
boys

Tess

"Yeah...so, uh, you got any hidden talents besides saving rockstar reputations?" Brad's flirty tone strokes warmth up my neck despite the harmless subject change.

I consider playing up some sexy mysterious persona but genuineness bubbles up instead. "Hmm, does extreme clumsiness count as a talent? I once sprained my wrist falling off a chair trying to change a lightbulb."

Brad's surprised laugh rewards my candor. "Now that sounds like story time."

I grin, settling deeper under the warm covers, suddenly wishing I wasn't alone. Rarely do I let professional walls down, yet something about this man keeps me reaching past the need for faultless control. "Maybe if you're lucky I'll demonstrate my gracelessness in person someday."

"I'll hold you to that," Brad volleys smoothly, the edge returning. Pleasant tension simmers down the line.

His next question surprises me. "You always this passionate about helping people reach success?"

I pause, debating keeping things light. I'm not sure how much I want to reveal about myself here. But late nights pave the way for truthfulness.

"Honestly? I sort of just drifted into publicity work. My teenage rebellion was more like mocking government in a debate club rather than singing in a band." I smile softly at the memory. "But I guess I still found ways to have a voice."

"Sounds pretty badass to me," Brad chuckles. "Taking on the system at a young age."

I grin at his praise. "I don't know about that. It wasn't as punk rock as it sounds. But I think it shaped my drive to understand different perspectives and help smooth communication." I hesitate before admitting, "This music world is very new for me. But the passion behind it - that connects universally, doesn't it?"

"No doubt about that," Brad agrees thoughtfully. "You gotta fight for whatever it is that makes you feel alive..." His voice trails off, perhaps remembering his own defining sparks.

I curl into my pillow, embracing this glimpse beyond Brad's image to the thoughtful soul I'm coming to know. I have a craving to know more. To know all about him. "What lit that fire in you? To become a rockstar, I mean?" I ask gently, unsure if he'll withdraw behind his walls again. I've noticed that in person, he does that, just like me.

But Brad surprises me with raw truth. "Honestly?

Rage. And having nothing to lose." He pauses thoughtfully. "Grew up in a pretty volatile place. Music was my escape from the shitshow at home. Lyrics in songs said things I couldn't find words for yet, you know?"

I hug my knees, my heart aching at the glimpse of pain in his words. "Like it gave you a voice when no one else listened."

"Yeah exactly," Brad sighs. "First guitar was just an old beater with crap strings that shredded my fingers trying to play. But I kept going till my hands bled night after night. Because for once I felt in control, shaping that pain into something beautiful."

I find myself holding back tears, awed by his early resilience to transform his hardship into something else through the power of creativity.

He continues softly. "Then I started writing my own messy songs and realized maybe someone out there might need a voice too. Need to not feel so alone." His voice cracks slightly. "If I help even one person struggling through something to feel some sort of hope...I don't know. My shitty story would maybe have meaning."

Emotion swells inside of me, understanding the redemptive purpose this dream has become for him. I whisper, "I really hope you get to achieve that goal."

"Me too."

A comforting understanding wraps around us in the thoughtful quiet. My thumb catches a stray tear as I keep our conversation on his side of the wall between us that shrinks by the minute. "Sounds like you found positive purpose, even if the journey had painful stops along the way."

"Trying to, yeah," Brad sighs raggedly into the phone. "Just want to use the platform for good, you know? Especially now seeing it all through Charlie's eyes. Wondering what kind of world she'll grow up in." He pauses. "What about you? Had any moments define the path you're on now?"

I steel myself, then whisper past the lump in my throat, "Well, watching my parent's vicious divorce kind of shaped my worldview early too." I squeeze my eyes shut debating opening old wounds so freely. Something about Brad makes me feel safe but caution still nags at me. Once words escape into stark reality, I can't take them back. I can't armor up my vulnerabilities again if things get messy later.

My breath catches sharply. Sensing my hesitation, Brad's gentle tone blankets my spiraling anxiety. "Hey, it's okay...we all got our own shit, you know? No pressure to unlock anything before you're ready."

His patience thaws my paralyzing doubts. This glimpse beyond his image reveals someone hurting, or who's been hurt, who understands holding back when stakes feel high. That solidarity steadies me to continue softly. "I guess figuring out how to be the emotional mediator, empathize, smooth constant drama and bull-shit just stuck with me. Became skills I built on for what-ever career path eventually clicked I guess."

I picture Brad nodding thoughtfully across whatever miles separate us. The understanding in his voice when he responds unfurls a warmth inside my chest, soothing old aches. "Makes sense why you're so damn good at this PR thing then," He offers quietly. "Taking turmoil and smoothing it into something good."

I flush, unexpectedly emotional at his praise reframing my old scars into strengths. "Well, that's still yet to be seen. I haven't exactly worked any miracles for you guys."

"Yet."

My smile is automatic, and I'm trying desperately to ignore the alarm bells going off in my head about this guy. But something happened on this call out of the blue. I think I got to know the real Brad Chambers. The one nobody else gets to see.

And I like it. I *really* like it.

"Yet," I echo.

As Brad opens up about his winding journey, this vulnerability reveals so much more beneath the surface to appreciate...and want.

And I know I'm in serious trouble.

My eyelids grow heavy, the glow of my bedside clock slowly registering through the cocoon we've built together in these dark hours. I should let Brad get some sleep, but ending this soulful glimpse behind his image and going back to a guarded distance tomorrow suddenly seems unbearable.

Can we maintain this magnetism in real life? Or is this it? Tomorrow we're back to how it was.

That thought slices through the warm bubble abruptly. My breath stutters picturing our professional bridges burned over reckless lines crossed way too soon. Am I ready to upend the stability I've scrambled for because my heart goes crazy whenever Brad Chambers is nearby? Could someone like him, who is so conditioned to run, ever outpace his ghosts for good and embrace something real?

The questions swirling dizzyingly are too dangerous to reconcile tonight. I force a steadiness I don't quite feel back into my voice, fingers already regretfully reaching to end the call.

"Guess I better let you rest up for the big audition day tomorrow." I bite my lip anxiously awaiting his response through the weighted silence.

I hear Brad shifting, his tone laced with the same reluctance holding me back. "Yeah, lots still to figure out." He pauses, words laden with meaning. "But thank you, Tess...for everything tonight."

My pulse flutters dangerously at the unspoken words neither of us dare give life to yet. "Sleep well, Rockstar," I whisper before disconnecting us from the intimate space we created.

I set my phone aside gently, skin still prickling from the force of words left unsaid. As I curl onto my own pillow, exhaustion eventually wins out over the fear and longing warring inside me at this uncharted new complication with Brad.

My dreams wander into dangerous territory - rough hands and ragged hearts seen through new eyes...

eleven
strangelove

Brad

My foot taps impatiently as we wait for this Dakota guy to show up. Charlie's going on and on trying to guess what cool accessories he might have. I'm only catching some of it though. I'm too distracted replaying Tess and me spilling our guts last night on the phone.

Did we cross lines getting that real about shit we don't normally tell people? Will she backpedal into polite small talk today keeping it strictly business now?

Or maybe she'll dodge personal shit altogether after going deep about family troubles and all. Keep any talk clipped to new bass player logistics and avoiding our chemistry altogether.

My stomach twists with nerves. I scrub a hand over my face, confusion mounting when Charlie asks, "You worried Dakota might suck too, huh Dad?"

"Hmm...? Oh, yeah..." I ruffle her hair, my mind spinning miles away. Man, I wish filterless kid drama was the biggest complication I had to deal with today. "Though, if he does, don't say it like that."

I rake my fingers through my hair, irritation building because for some reason it matters if Tess acts distant after we spilled our souls. Why do I care if she throws walls up protecting herself after our talk last night? Don't I do the same damn thing? Have I?

I start bouncing my knee, anxiety spiking as I hear the door creak open, and her heels click towards us. But my breath catches seeing her features tighten subtly noticing my fidgeting. Her smile seems to dim behind the polite professionalism she must have built back up overnight.

I wish I could do that.

Before disappointment sinks in, she ducks her head almost shyly. "Hey...about last night, hope I didn't over-share too much. Just easy to talk to you I guess."

Relief floods me as her words poke holes in my worries. My lips quirk up teasingly. "Please, tell me more about how you apparently took down Congress in high school debate club. That's the story I'm waiting on."

Tess's eyes light up, shoulders relaxing as she laughs. "Well, if Dakota's audition goes sideways today, I'm clearly the secret weapon here. Just let me at him."

Our banter dissolves any lingering awkwardness. Maybe navigating the blurred lines feels less complicated in the light of day after all. Without dissecting it too much, we seem to have picked up where we left off. That brief intimate glimpse bound us in a new understanding of each other.

It's an intimacy I've never let myself feel before with anyone I've been with. Everything before now has been 'what you see is what you get.' There's never been a question as to the *why* of any of it. Or if there was, I never wanted to share that part of me.

With Tess, it's different. One fucking phone call, and my life is suddenly upside down and inside out.

The door suddenly swings open again, grabbing everyone's attention. Dakota strides in eagerly with a guitar case in one hand, and my blushing daughter's enthusiastic hand in the other. Guess she snagged first dibs on access behind that mystery beanie waiting outside. Tess and I share surprised, hopeful glances at this unexpected start.

Charlie drags Dakota over, grinning ear to ear. "His beanie has skull flowers, isn't that so cool?"

Dakota ducks his head almost bashfully as we take him in. I can't deny his talent flashing through the video we saw held intrigue, and now seeing his humble but reserved confidence in person, I'm actually hopeful.

"Well, the lady has spoken. You're clearly crushing the audition already," I joke, breaking the ice. Dakota laughs, a musicality in it echoing throughout the space. As if buoyed by the positivity, he makes eye contact with each of us.

"I know I'm probably not what you had in mind. But thanks for taking a chance..." He trails off, waiting for our cues.

I glance at Tess, reading the silent encouragement there to drop any remaining skepticism. She's right.

Hidden gems show up in unexpected packages sometimes.

"Hey man, only thing that matters to us is if you can bring the fire. The video glimpses were solid." I extend my hand, an offer to wipe slates clean and feel him out with impartial ears. "I'm Brad. Your biggest fan's dad."

Dakota's grin spreads slowly as he shakes my hand. He turns to lift his guitar respectfully. "Well, I'm definitely eager to jam together. I'm probably Chaos Fuel's biggest fan, so this is huge."

Everyone is introduced, and we start in on our audition songs. I cue the opening chords to a newer song. Dakota comes in tentatively at first, but then finds the bass groove. Hope flickers as we build on it with layers of guitar and drums.

Just as the musical alchemy starts to catch, Dakota flubs on a tempo change. Notes tumble disjointedly until he grimaces and cuts out.

I motion reassurance when he shoots an embarrassed look my way. "No problem, dude. Song's still fresh for all of us. Top again?" Dakota nods, exhaling unsteadily before Emmett counts us back in. Desperation edges into my encouragement despite my best efforts. "Let's keep the energy light, yeah? No pressure."

I flash a strained, rallying smile Dakota's way, even as doubt plagues my thoughts.

Come on...ignite that spark we glimpsed already. Find the pocket again, man.

Feeling the guys' eyes boring impatient judgment into Dakota's back beside me grates on my last nerve.

Should I send them off, give Dakota air to breathe? Or will that shake his confidence even more somehow?

My temples throb as I strain to keep my game face steady. But it's one thing soothing Charlie's artistic growing pains. Faking unwavering faith as I watch the wheels falling off something everything's riding on now is totally different. Raw panic is dangerously close to erupting.

I just gotta buy some time for Dakota to shake off the jitters and showcase himself. If that magic still fucking exists to find... Before the guys revolt or the label pulls the plug on this whole experiment.

We regain momentum, but Dakota seems distracted now, overthinking. His tentative playing gets eclipsed behind our swell. I feel the tires spinning out again before it happens.

He hesitates on a bass fill then overcompensates missing the drop back in completely. Dakota yelps as his shoe catches on an unplugged cable and he nearly face-plants. Whatever band chemistry was building visibly fractures.

Irritation bubbles inside at the unraveling disaster now happening that I feared was coming. Dakota shrinks under our collective impatience. But Charlie just calls out happily, "That was a cool dance move!"

Charlie's innocent praise lightens the mood slightly after Dakota's stumbling mishaps. But underlying doubt gnaws at me whether we can resolve his issues in time for tour, let alone live shows. Still, I force a gentler tone addressing him.

"Hey man, first days jamming are always awkward, you know? Why don't we try an older one next to get our bearings?" I nod subtly toward Stefan and Emmett too, signaling them to tone down the intensity that's obviously intimidating Dakota further.

I count us smoothly off into an old favorite, relieved when Dakota grasps the familiar progression. His shoulders loosen up incrementally, though he avoids eye contact still. As the final chords ring out, I manage an encouraging smile his way.

"See, you got this. We'll take it slow..." My confidence wanes watching Dakota's embarrassed flush not fade though. The other guys hover impatiently just out of his sight line.

Tess reads the scenario unraveling and jumps in. "You know, I'd love to grab some behind-the-scenes photos documenting this pivotal day." She gestures vaguely. "Why don't you three take Dakota through some gear while I set up lighting?"

The guys exchange skeptical looks but follow her lead and drift off. I mouth grateful thanks Tess's way. She gives a subtle thumbs up before tactfully busying herself scoping out creative shots to explain away giving Dakota some space. Hopefully once nerves settle, his abilities shine through.

But my gut twists seeing how badly this first impression is going off the rails. I pray inwardly that this instinct to take a chance here doesn't backfire on us all.

I desperately try to tune out the doubtful looks that get exchanged as we give Dakota some space. If we all seem on edge too, it'll only feed his unraveling confidence more.

After reviewing gear and lighting angles just to kill time, we circle back. I grab the mic again, determined to keep spirits hopeful.

"Alright Dakota, no second guesses now. What do you say we just jam loose and see what flows? No rules. No wrong notes. Just make some fucking noise together."

I see a flicker reignite behind his averted eyes at the freedom I just offered. As Stefan lays down a mood-setting rhythmic riff, Dakota closes his eyes. His head bobs along slowly finding the pocket again.

He starts layering in subtle bass notes accenting Stefan's. Building off each other, no plan in mind, creative sparks tentatively realign. Emmett taps a gentle beat and Stefan weaves textured guitar riffs through it.

We meander along improvisationally before Dakota suddenly infuses a slick bass slide leading toward a key change. Our sound shifts following his unexpected modulation. Bursts of rhythmic runs and riffs tumble out, answering each other.

The studio fills with our unified sound gelling fully at last. Dakota no longer shrinks but flows freely as part of us. No more thought, just instinctive reaction to rhythms and notes circling endlessly.

It's a fucking miracle.

I meet Tess's eyes glowing with relief as she snaps photos, capturing the moment. In this unguarded creative space, Dakota transformed. I guess raw talent and collaborative magic can't stay buried for long after all.

We've found our guy.

Over burgers later, it's just us band guys and Tess debriefing Dakota's audition.

"Kid seemed to gel with your vibe decently after that shaky start, yeah?" Ian asks, stealing a fry off my plate. "Didn't try outplaying anybody, just blended right in."

"Yeah, he rode the improv waves pretty smoothly once we gave him room," I agree. "Talent's there behind the shaggy hair for sure."

Tess smiles supportively. "You're right. The musicality and humility shone through. Fans will definitely take to that."

Emmett gestures enthusiastically, mouth full. "So, we dig Dingdong right?" Crumbs spray as he fumbles Dakota's name.

We share amused glances at the mangled moniker. Stefan lifts his soda, expression assessing. "He's young but held his own against our sound well enough. Eventually."

"Young and eager balances out old and cynical sometimes," Ian reasons, tone thoughtful as we each process our own perspectives.

I meet Tess's eyes, sensing she reads my wavelength here. The technical skills and collaborative style that Dakota brought to the table click effortlessly with how we create. There's no sense chasing hypothetical perfection and risking the organic band magic that seems to be brewing here. Catching improbable lightning in a bottle like this feels destined somehow.

Strange how people step into your path right when you need them most.

That might be happening a lot lately.

"So, I found a bass player!" Charlie sing-songs as she skips over, her face beaming. "You said I could help, and I found the bestest one. His name is Dee-koda."

I stifle a laugh at her garbled pronunciation. "You sure did good, baby girl. We all think Dakota might just be the musical brother we've been missing."

"Told you his flower beanie was epic, and he had talent," Charlie gloats playfully. Then curiosity sparks. "Is Dakota our family now then, if he's your brother?"

The innocent connection catches me off guard. I meet Tess's surprised yet touched eyes again across the table at Charlie's leap, embracing Dakota so immediately.

Something unspoken passes between us as our eyes catch, acknowledging that family comes in unexpected forms. I know welcoming in people fate-scarred and bent like us feels right.

I hold Tess's gaze a beat too long, that startling soul connection sparking to life once more. Her lips part slightly, hesitation and longing warring in her expression. Does she feel the same terrifying thrill I do? That we might be misfit pieces of the same ragged puzzle somehow?

Stefan's soda can pops loudly next to me, snapping

the spell. I force my attention reluctantly back to Charlie still chattering brightly beside me "...and we can have family band night with pizza parties now, too."

Tess ducks her head with a shy smile as I smooth Charlie's hair. "Yeah, I'm sure Dakota will be happy being part of our creative family."

I meet Tess's eyes fleetingly once more, electricity still crackling unfinished between us despite the broken intimacy. An unspoken understanding lingers between us. Possibilities and boundaries are blurring. Where this all leads remains frighteningly uncertain, but I like this feeling.

"Right," Ian says, rolling into motion. "If we're all in agreement then? I'll get Eliza on the line to get this finalized."

Glancing at Emmett and Stefan to confirm, we all nod at each other. The weight that's been on our shoulders visibly lifts as we all let out deep breaths.

I stand and pull Charlotte up, twirling her around in circles. "Let the chaos begin."

twelve
where to begin

Tess

I slide my tablet into its case, stealing glances at Brad gathering things on the other side of the studio. His worn leather jacket hangs distractingly over a nearby chair. My fingers can't help but trail along the buttery soft material as I pass, imagining the warmth remaining from his body heat.

Caught up in the tactile memory, I don't notice Brad moving around until we nearly collide next to the door.

"Whoa, sorry!" His hands catch my elbows, igniting the inches between us.

My breath hitches being wrapped in his faded cologne so close. Smokey gray eyes lift to hold mine, our push-pull tension suddenly crackling in the confined space. I sway unconsciously nearer, forgetting all the professional lines we blurred during our phone call last night.

"It's okay..." I exhale.

Just then Charlie bursts in and the sensual haze

dissolves. Brad's fiery gaze drops abruptly, but the electric undercurrent remains brewing between us.

"Dad, did June's dad tell you I'm sleeping over tonight?" Charlie runs around in a whirl of sparkles and red curls.

Brad blinks in surprise at the sudden change of plans as she tugs on his sleeve. "Uh no, guess it slipped Ian's mind mentioning that little detail..."

"So now you have the whole night off!" Charlie announces brightly. Then her expression turns scheming beyond her years. "You can take Tess on a date."

My eyes dart to Brad's, pulse hammering, but he just coughs out an awkward laugh. "Baby girl, I'm sure Tess already has plans."

His apologetic glance sends a secret thrill through me as Charlie's bubbly playing holds momentum. "No, she doesn't. She's free too. Aren't you Tess? Pleeeease say you'll have dinner with my daddy." The wide-eyed Disney princess turns her charms in my direction.

I bite my lip, hesitating only briefly as warmth rushes into my cheeks. Guess there's only one possible response to such a sweet matchmaking attempt. I meet Brad's gaze. "Well apparently my evening is wide open now..."

Brad rakes a hand through his hair, something unreadable shifting in his eyes as Charlie awaits my response expectantly.

"Dinner would be great," I say, hints of a shy smile emerging. Brad studies me for a lingering moment before amusement finally claims victory over whatever silent debate just happened behind his inscrutable expression.

"Alright troublemaker, let's get you over to this surprise sleepover then so you're not late." Brad scoops a protesting Charlie up, chuckling as he tickles her. Their giggles wash away any remaining tension between us.

He meets my eyes over Charlie's shoulder warmly. "Meet you back here in an hour? I know a place nearby we can walk to, best barbecue in the city."

My grin spreads slowly picturing a glimpse into Brad's world beyond these studio walls. "That sounds perfect actually. It's a date." The enthusiasm bubbles out before I can let any second thoughts creep in.

Brad's eyes crease with an echoing smile that quickens my pulse and lingers long after they've disappeared through the door with a giggling Charlie.

I've got a date with Brad Chambers.

Holy shit.

My hands tremble slightly swiping on a layer of mascara. Brad Chambers waiting for a date across town and I'm freaking out like a teenager again.

When my phone lights up with Ivy's face, I pounce gratefully. "Help, I panicked and wore my maroon blouse, black jeans. Too dressy? Too boring?" I ramble anxiously.

My best friend squeals through the line. "You landed a hot date and didn't tell me? Spill. I want all the tea."

I smile despite the maelstrom raging in my head. Ivy listens eagerly as I dish about the crazy audition details ending with surprise matchmaker Charlie's proposal. "So now I'm dressing like a soccer mom about to seduce a rockstar."

Ivy coos affectionately. "Honey, that man won't care if you wear a paper bag. Just let him see that shining spirit underneath. Wear a red lace bra for inspiration, though - and easy access."

I flush wildly imagining such presumptuousness. Will tonight be more than just dinner conversation? How far am I willing to take this?

My muscles coil tightly wondering if I'm ready for wherever my impulsiveness might lead if romance knocks our guarded walls down for good.

"It's just...this is the textbook rebound fling scenario, right? Maybe I'm still reeling about Corey?" I nibble my thumbnail as I pace, phone squeezed between my shoulder and ear.

"Girl, you dumped him. And good riddance," she snaps. "Besides, that was months ago. His name hasn't even come up since then until you just said it. It's not that at all."

She's right, of course. It's not rebound. I'm just freaking the hell out.

"Okay, but this is a rockstar we're talking about here. I know better than to get sucked in when the writing's basically tattooed on the bathroom wall already."

Ivy sighs sympathetically. "The heart wants what it wants, babe. Maybe the beauty is embracing the wild ride for however long it lasts. No regrets."

I smile softly despite the cartwheeling nerves in my

gut. "Look at you, getting all Zen on me. But seriously, can I risk the fallout here? Jeopardizing the client relationship with the label if this crashes and burns? And where does Charlie even fit in?" My breath hitches as I focus on all the confusing emotions.

"Okay, valid worries," Ivy soothes. "But that precious girl clearly ships you two together. So, I say slip on that red lace for luck and let yourself be swept away on the tidal wave already pulling you under. The answers will come in time if it's meant to be."

"It's just...I could jeopardize everything I've built if things crash and burn here. I can barely keep my focus straight whenever Brad is in my general vicinity. People will notice how unprofessional I get." I sigh, flopping back on a pile of discarded tops strewn on the bed.

Ivy makes an exaggerated sound of enlightenment. "Oh, now we get to the real inner turmoil. Girl's got it bad for Rockstar Daddy..."

I lift my head to glare at the phone. "Don't call him that. But yeah, you're not wrong." I cover my flushed face in embarrassment.

"Hey, ain't no shame in that game. Just shows you're human. I'm sure you can set reasonable boundaries when needed." Ivy's breezy reassurance smooths my ruffled feathers.

I twist a lock of hair thoughtfully. "It's just...I catch his eye sometimes and forget what I was even doing. Those smoldering looks short circuit my damn brain." I laugh softly, nerves ebbing to cautious excitement again.

"But yeah, hopefully some professionalism kicks back in when I have to actually work."

Ivy giggles triumphantly. "See, you got this. Now go rock his world."

My eyes squeeze shut as I exhale slowly, letting her advice seep in. Maybe she's right. Resistance against the untamable is exhausting. I grab my faded leather jacket as anticipation flutters dangerously across my heart. "Well, here goes nothing. Time to go catch that wave and see where it carries me. Wish me luck."

"Good luck!" she sings.

Damn her encouragement.

My boot heels click on the asphalt as I make my way toward Brad's car, fresh nerves and excitement running riotously within my chest. *Get it together*, I remind myself. *This is just two adults sharing a casual meal.*

Except my pep talk does little to calm the inner swarm of butterflies that have resurfaced as I take in Brad leaning against the gleaming hood of his car. His rolled-up sleeves showcase tattooed forearms that always seem to quicken my pulse. The one of the word *CHAOS* especially poignant given the circumstances.

As he looks up to greet me with that magnetic smile though, the atmosphere shifts subtly. Gone is the distant rockstar front he usually puts on to conceal the real him. Tonight, it's just Brad meeting my gaze, open and at ease in a way I've only glimpsed in a few unguarded moments before.

He straightens from his casual lean against the car as I approach, eyes glinting warmly beneath the amber streetlights.

"Hey there. Wasn't sure if you'd really show up after Charlie pulled that whole matchmaker thing earlier." He combs back his hair with his fingers, awkwardness creeping in as we hover on the precipice of date territory neither of us expected.

I smooth my blouse self-consciously, going for light-hearted recovery. "Are you kidding? Getting the inside scoop on the best hole-in-the-wall barbecue dive in town? I'd have to be crazy to turn that down."

The small insertion of humor dissolves the tension a little as we fall into step together, shoulders brushing occasionally. Brad's fingers drift tentatively toward mine, and I soften my hand into his, savoring the warm connection kindling to life on this unexpected evening full of possibility neither of us planned on...yet somehow feels fated at the same time.

Our linked hands swing lazily between us, perfectly in tune with each stride down the fading sidewalk. No pressure exists to fill silences that feel as easy as our private laughter. Still, I crave to know more of the layers beneath Brad's polished facade.

"So, tell me...how does the great Brad Chambers actually unwind on his nights off?" I ask.

Brad chuckles low under the flickering streetlights. "I've become pretty boring honestly. Just average stuff like browsing songs or videos, having a beer or two. Maybe hitting a show on the strip if friends are playing."

I tilt my head thoughtfully. "What? No wild hot tub parties on super yachts overflowing with models?"

He snorts, playing along. "You found my schedule, huh? Nah, the rockstar perks get old quick. These days I just need good company, and that's hard to come by." His eyes hold mine meaningfully before darting away shyly.

I glimpse the real man so few have earned access to and savor his trust opening up. Hand squeezed gently, I redirect playfully to keep things light. "Well, I'll try my best. We have incredible barbecue and my sparkling conversation to look forward to."

Soon we're nestled in a cozy corner booth, chatting easily as we await our food. I hesitate, but curiosity wins out. "So, even though things didn't work out romantically, it seems you and Ren made things really positive for Charlie as co-parents. Was that always smooth sailing?"

Brad nods thoughtfully, taking a sip of his beer. "Honestly, things got messy for a while after the split. But we finally realized Charlie had to come first. Well, *I* finally realized it. I wasn't exactly a model father in the beginning. Once Jude came along, he helped mellow the drama."

"That's really great you worked through things for her sake." I smile gently, the shadow in his eyes at old regrets achingly familiar. I redirect playfully before melancholy can creep in. "What about you though? Still fighting off groupies?"

I don't know why I keep bringing up groupies.

Maybe because in my research of the band, it's all I saw with Brad. One after the other, and some even on repeat. Deep down, it's a real fear that it's the only relationship he can have. If it is, my heart is about to get broken.

Brad's eyes sparkle reading me clearly. "Well, there may be a few still trying their luck, but I'm pretty focused on just one incredible woman lately."

A surprised smile spreads across my face as Brad's fingers interlace with mine across the checked tablecloth between us.

"Oh, is that so?" I arch a teasing brow, heart racing. "She must really be something to keep the infamous play-boy's attention away from all those glamorous temptations."

Brad's thumb traces distracting circles on my wrist as he leans in. "She's smart as hell, refreshing as a rainstorm in the desert...and so damn beautiful it hurts sometimes."

His poetic words dissolve my ability to volley any sort of witty quip back at him. Blushing, I glance down shyly before meeting his smoldering gaze again. "Well, hopefully she feels the same about you."

"I hope so too."

Our charged stare lingers, words unnecessary to convey the attraction amplifying with each revealed layer tonight. As tempting appetizers arrive, breaking the tension, I know I'm already in too deep falling for this beautiful man.

Way too deep. And, way too quickly.

The savory aroma of sizzling meat envelops us in this tucked away booth, cocooned from the outside world.

Lost in animated conversation, everything fades but this man whose smallest gestures transfix me. How his calloused fingertips skim my wrist bone idly during pauses...the heat of his steady gaze refusing to release mine each time our eyes catch.

My skin prickles, hyperaware of these electric undercurrents circulating stronger by the minute. I imagine the scratch of his beard I ache to feel grazing my neck. This exhilarating attraction threatens to ignite full force with each subtle shift closer beneath the low lighting of the restaurant.

"So will I get to enjoy more of your company when you're not fixing the next crisis of the week?" Brad asks lightly when finally locating stray words again.

But a smoldering tension arises in the understated question. My heart skips imagining how this magnetic pull between us might deepen. I wet my lips that have gone suddenly dry. "I'd really like that..."

thirteen
lucky

Brad

A reluctant sigh escapes as I meet Tess's eyes across the table of the booth we've nested in for hours now. As much as I want to cling to this moment, the deserted restaurant reminds me that closing time can't be too far off now.

My fingers drift distractedly along her forearm, tracing nonsense shapes and letters. Part of me still can't believe how fast everything clicked into place once we stopped overthinking it all. Witnessing Tess so at ease, engaging with *me*, not some pre-conceived image she's conjured of me in her head, eclipses any remaining *what-if* doubts.

Now new, more dangerous questions creep in. Like how difficult resisting the magnetic urge to capture her lips will prove walking her back to the studio. Or how long taking things slow and steady will last. I'm not exactly one to pace myself. Not when I want something.

Or *someone*.

Because I know one taste of her won't satisfy what rapidly is going to grow into an insatiable hunger once I start. My restless hands itch, wanting to map every supple curve of hers.

But I can't screw this up. For once my impatience can't rule or push her trust too far too fast. This woman deserves to be handled with care as I peel back each hypnotic layer, blinding and wrecking me further.

"Looks like we've closed the place," Tess says, reluctantly leaning back and sliding out of reach. Her eyes sparkle like she's just woken up from a dream.

If this is a dream, I don't want to wake up.

"Guess so," I say, not wanting this date to end. It's hard to hide my disappointment.

Her hands slide around my waist as we walk, moving up from holding hands, and I can only stand having her so close for one block before I have to stop.

Under the glow of a streetlight, I turn her to face me, her eyes are bright and questioning, searching mine. *God, she's gorgeous.* Pushing through my sudden nerves, I run my thumb along her soft cheek and ask, "Can I kiss you?"

She hesitates for a second, but smiles. "I wish you w—"

I don't let her finish, and brush my lips against hers gently, stealing her words, the warmth of her breath mingling with mine so sweetly. But it's not enough.

I don't want the sweet, I want the fire. I want more.

Delving deeper into the kiss, I pull her closer just as she pulls me in, meeting in the middle where there's nothing left between us. Our guards are fully down, and the taste of her is exactly as perfect as I imagined.

My fingers run through her silky hair as her hands slide up my back under my jacket. She leans into the kiss, leans into me, and it's all I can do not to grind against her. She's stirring physical reactions in me that are undeniable, but way too early to consider.

I would love nothing more than to take her home and see this through, but I've already sworn to myself to take this slow. This can't be like the rest. Tess isn't like anybody else.

This is special.

I dig somewhere deep inside for strength I didn't know I had and force myself to release the kiss, putting an inch or two between us. We're both breathless, and as I gaze at Tess, her lips slightly swollen from the kiss, I have to fight myself not to dive in for more.

She blinks a few times, as if clearing her mind from a fog. "Whoa."

"Whoa, indeed," I chuckle, smoothing her hair that I've messed up during the kiss. "Sorry. I couldn't help myself. I've been wanting to do that for days." The admission slips out without thinking, and I internally kick myself for being so transparent.

"Days?" she asks, amused.

I sigh. The cat's out of the bag, may as well feed it. "Yup. When I first met you, I knew you'd be trouble."

Her amusement turns into confusion. "*I'd* be trouble? How?"

"I knew that if I got close, I'd get burned."

The crease between her brows deepens. "Burned?"

"You've definitely set me on fire," I admit, leaning down to kiss her again, and it's a slow, meaningful exchange that expresses exactly what has been set ablaze inside of me since we met.

When I pull away this time, it's even harder to do than the last time. This is insane. The emotions that are rolling through me the longer I spend time with Tess are going to overwhelm me. I'm not used to feeling this much outside of when I'm on stage. In fact, this feels a lot like that. Nobody has ever made me feel this way.

"Well, damn," Tess whispers, her eyes opening slowly to meet mine. When they do, that electric connection between us sparks brighter again. "How much wine did I actually have?"

"Are you feeling drunk?" Now I'm worried I just took advantage of her.

She laughs, and it sounds like a song. "Not really. But that kiss sure is making me question things."

I wrap my arms around her and pull her close, inhaling her perfume, making a mental note to memorize this moment. This feeling. Everything about it.

"Don't question anything about this," I murmur into her hair. "I'm not. For once."

She tilts her head up to me. "For once?"

A wry smile escapes. "I usually question everything and everyone. There are usually ulterior motives for people wanting to be in my orbit. With you, I'm not doing that. I'm not questioning it."

"Well, don't I feel special?" She laughs, and I know

she's trying to lighten the mood. I did get pretty serious, pretty quickly. Maybe I should go easy.

"You are." I just can't shut up, can I? For fuck's sake. "Sorry, the moonlight's getting to me."

She gives me a small squeeze. "No, please. Go on. This is giving me life."

"Nah, it's going to start going to your head."

We start walking again, still holding on to each other as we laugh and tease each other. But as we turn into the parking lot of the studio I freeze in my tracks. Someone is leaning on my car, waiting for me. My blood runs cold.

Gina. My ex.

Fuck.

"What is it...?" Tess's question trails off as she sees what's made me stop so suddenly. "Oh."

I don't like the tone in her voice, as if she expected something like this to happen. And I really don't like that I've somehow managed to meet that expectation.

"It's my ex," I explain, though if she's done any research on me, like she says she has, she already knows this. And she'll know that it was a volatile relationship at the best of times.

She starts to pull out from under my arm, "I know. I should go..."

"No. Don't," I plead, pulling her back to my side, and whispering into her ear. "Please."

Her body stiffens, but then relaxes against me. She doesn't say anything, but nods, keeping her eyes trained on my ex warily.

We approach Gina, who has her arms crossed over her chest, and a glare that could kill if I let it.

"We need to talk, Brad," she says, flicking her long dark hair over her shoulder as she gives Tess a rude once over.

"Actually, we don't," I say, pulling Tess tighter against me, trying to be reassuring. This is not what I wanted to deal with on our first date. Or ever. "We had our final 'talk' months ago. I'm pretty sure nothing was left out."

"But I've changed. I swear," she says, demeanor shifting swiftly. Too quickly. She pushes off the car, and I can see in the overhead light from the nearby door that her eyes are glassy.

Shit. She's on something.

Tess must notice me go rigid as Gina approaches because her arm around me tightens.

"Who's this? My replacement?" Gina shoots another glare at Tess as she steps closer.

I instinctively move to place myself between them. Gina is a hot head to begin with, and if she's high, who the fuck knows what she's capable of.

"You need to leave," I say, wanting to get this confrontation over with as soon as possible. She's already ruined the best date I've ever had. "We have nothing left to say to each other."

"I'm pregnant."

My stomach drops. If it's true, I know it's not mine. We haven't been together in at least six months. And if she's really strung out while she's pregnant...*Jesus Christ.*

"Give Bobby my congratulations." That's who she cheated on me with, and who, I assume, is the father.

"Funny," she chuckles. "He said the same about you when he dropped me off here."

"Well, we both know it's not mine. So, go back to Bobby, and have a nice life with your family. Leave me and mine alone."

"You're being so mean. When did you get so mean?" She reaches out for me, but I step backward, careful to move Tess with me, keeping my spot between them.

I don't like the crazy vibe emanating from Gina right now, and I need to diffuse the situation quicker than I am doing.

"Seriously. Congratulations to you both. I hope you're happy," I say, trying to be sincere, even though I feel like I'm spitting out venom. I was so stupid to ever think I wanted this woman. She got clean when she was with me. It's sad to see what she's become since. "Now, please, just leave me alone."

Before she can respond or reach out again, a car peels into the parking lot, radio blasting. They screech to a stop behind my car.

Bobby.

The window rolls down and smoke pours out, revealing my supposed former nemesis. One I couldn't give two shits about now.

"Get in the fucking car, Gina," he orders sharply.

I step back again, pulling Tess tight next to me, signaling to Gina that I am not an option for her, and she needs to deal with her own shit.

"But you're being an asshole," she whines, stomping her foot like a child.

"Just get in the fucking car," he replies, rolling his eyes at her.

She glances back at Tess and I and must see that she doesn't have a lot of choice in the matter. I get the feeling her being here was part of a bigger game they're both playing with each other. One I definitely want no part of.

"Fine," she pouts, and rounds the car to get in.

As they pull out of the parking lot, I don't release the breath I've been holding until the car is out of sight, and I think Tess does the same.

"Well, that's one way to make a first date memorable, huh?" I say, deflated now that the night's been ruined by my ex.

"Um...yeah. That's pretty unforgettable." Her tone is surprisingly light. Maybe things aren't ruined after all.

"I'm sorry about that." I really am at a loss for what to say after a display like that. I'm still reeling a bit.

"Don't apologize. That was obviously not your fault."

I can feel the relief wash over me in a wave. "You're amazing," I say, kissing her forehead. "I hate to end our date on that sour note, though."

She turns her head toward the studio suggestively. "It doesn't have to end yet."

I'm digging the studio keys out of my pocket before I take another breath, pulling her along with me toward the building.

"Then it won't."

fourteen
only love

Tess

I'm not sure what I was thinking when I suggested the date didn't have to end. The last few minutes have left me dizzy, and I don't think it's all made sense yet.

Brad shuts the door behind me, then pins me with his hands flat against it above my shoulders. I'm caged, and he's so close. His spicy cologne is intoxicating. He leans in for a kiss and I respond automatically, drowning in the sensations as his mouth hungrily takes mine.

As the kiss breaks, and his lips start to travel down my neck with delicious precision, my body wants to give in to him. Throw myself into this passionate moment.

But my mind is revolting.

"Wait," I whisper, gently pushing him away.

He immediately stops and straightens, running a hand through his hair.

"Sorry. Sorry." He turns away and goes to the mini fridge for a beer, opening it quickly and taking a swig.

I'm still leaning against the door, trying to catch my breath. Trying to reign in all my scattered thoughts and emotions. I can only imagine what he's going through.

"No, I'm sorry," I say, stepping over and grabbing the beer from him, taking my own long pull before handing it back. It earns me an arched brow that's laced with a few emotions I can't quite identify.

"Why are you sorry?"

"I just..." It takes me a second to find the words. "I'm not sure why I suggested coming in here, after..."

"After the bullshit with my ex." It's obvious he's angry. And he has every right to be. I would be in his place.

"Maybe we should talk about what happened out there?" I round the couch and sit down, patting the cushion next to me for him to sit, and he does, letting out a long sigh.

"Well, as I said, that was my ex, Gina," he grimaces just saying her name. "I haven't seen or heard anything from her in like six or seven months. She cheated on me with the douchebag who picked her up, Bobby."

"I know who she is," I say flatly. I've seen her pictures while doing my research, and she's even prettier in person. Messed up as hell, but still pretty. I can feel the jealousy creeping in and push it away. "And she's supposedly pregnant?"

"So she says..." Another frown creases his brow, his eyes now haunted.

"You don't believe her?"

His anger flares again. "I don't know. She used that

to get me back once before when we were fighting. She claimed she lost it after a few weeks, but it turns out she was never pregnant. Her best friend told me the truth after the fact."

"Holy shit. How could she do that?"

"Who fucking knows why anyone does anything? She also got clean when we were together. I guess that's a thing of the past. She looked high as a fucking kite out there."

My stomach lurches, thinking if she is pregnant, what she's doing to her own body if she's using, let alone a baby too. It sickens me to think someone could be so manipulative. Especially to Brad who's already a father. They'd have to know what that meant to him.

"Why do you think she was here tonight?" I ask, still trying to make sense of the whole situation.

He sips his beer, his anger slowly subsiding. "That's the million-dollar question. I'm assuming they were fighting, and one of them thought to drag me into it. Either to make the other jealous or dump her off on me to make a statement."

"Lucky you," I say, taking the beer for another quick pull. "Does that happen a lot? Like with anyone else from your past?" I need to know if this is a recurring thing with Brad's exes. Sure, I've researched them, but nothing like this ever came up before. If I'm going to be playing ex-girlfriend whack-a-mole, I'd like to be prepared.

He hesitates before answering, and my chest clenches. I'm not going to like his answer, I can tell.

He glances at me, but doesn't meet my eyes, and looks away just as quickly. "That's hard to say. At least, kind of. Maybe. I don't know how to put it."

"Honesty would be great," I say sarcastically, handing the bottle back to him.

That gets his attention, and he meets my eyes, a storm raging in his steely grays.

"Tess, I'm being honest with you." He rubs at the stubble on his chin, annoyed. "I just don't know how to explain."

The blood in my veins is cooling, wondering what is so difficult about this. It should be an easy answer. Yes or no.

"Brad, I need to know if this is a regular thing. Do people from your past show up like this all the time?"

"Not all the time..."

I feel sick. "You're not giving me the warm fuzzies here." Thoughts of leaving now and moving on are running through my head. I guess it's better I found this out now before I got too invested in a relationship with him. But just the thought of ending this now craters my heart. Still, my spine straightens, ready to bolt.

He shifts to face me, his eyes now sad as if he knows what I'm thinking. "Listen. I can't predict what other people are going to do. Ever. And unfortunately, I do have a lot of people in my past. I can't deny that." He pauses, but I don't respond. "On occasion people pop up out of the blue, looking for another good time."

My breath still feels trapped in my throat. I knew he

used to be a playboy but didn't think it was still a thing. "Good time?"

His face flushes slightly. "It used to be my motto: 'I'm here for a good time, not a long time.'" He shakes his head ruefully, and I can see embarrassment, or maybe it's shame, coloring his features now. "It's just how it was."

"You say that like it's past tense. But is that what you're doing with me? Just looking for a good time, not a long time?"

"Absolutely not," he says quickly, and with a sternness I've not seen in him. He sets the bottle on the coffee table and grabs both of my hands in his. "This is different, Tess. This is way different."

His assurances hit the wall of doubt I've taken years to build brick by painful brick inside me though. I've heard that a million times before and been burned every time I believed it. *This is different.* Can someone conditioned to use charm as currency ever surrender the upper hand? Once the novelty fades, what stops his old instincts from kicking in, tossing aside promises to chase whatever next thrill comes around?

I shake my head, bitterness from old wounds festering. My ex Corey's lies that sounded so similar bounce around my weary heart. "People don't just flip an enlightenment switch and change their patterns, no matter how much we want to."

Brad's mouth tightens. I brace for predictable excuses or deflection. Instead, his jaw sets with an unfamiliar resolve. "You're absolutely right. I can't rewrite my past.

It is what it is. But I am willing to reshape my future." His eyes burn fervently now. "Or try to. I've been trying to. Just tell me what I need to do."

I want to believe him with every fiber of my being but doubts still shadow my thoughts. I, for one, know that people don't instantly change. And even if he's telling the truth, what happens when one of his 'good times' shows up when I'm not around? I don't know if I can handle a relationship like this.

I don't share. It's monogamy or nothing with me.

So, what do I do now? Cut and run? Or give him the benefit of the doubt, and see how it goes?

How much can my heart take?

fifteen
warning from my demons

Brad

Leave it to my fucking ex, Gina, to ruin what is possibly the best date I've ever had. Fucking hell. I finally met someone who I think understands me as a person. *Me.* The fuck up who is just trying his fucking best to make good. To make up for what an absolute shitstorm of a person I used to be. And she just pops up out of fucking nowhere and derails everything.

I can see in Tess's eyes that she doubts me now. I don't blame her. I *can't* blame her. My fucked-up reputation precedes me wherever I go. To be honest, I'm surprised we've gotten this far. Any sane person would have run away from me with their pants on fire.

But she's still here. In front of me. Wanting to believe me. It's plain as day that she wants to, but she's holding herself back. And it's killing me.

"I don't know what words I could possibly say to convince you I'm no longer like that," I start, as earnestly as I can. "But I'll die trying to find them. I swear."

"You don't have to—"

"Yes. Yes, I do." Despite her words, I can tell she's just being nice. Of course she is. She's Tess. But I need to explain myself. It's the only way to make this make sense to her. "This whole world is new to you, and let me tell you, it's not pretty. It's not glamorous. Sometimes it's the most depraved and dark side of people that you can imagine, and some you don't even want to picture. I've seen it. Hell, I even gave into it for a while. Too long." I run a hand through my hair, reaching for my beer again for comfort as I talk.

"It's easy to lose yourself, and who you are. It's easy to stop being a fucking person and just let your demons run free because everyone else is doing the same fucking thing. You don't see how messed up it is because you're right in the thick of it. You think, 'Well, this is how it is here,' when it's fucking not."

Her demeanor softens, and her empathy flows around and through me.

This woman.

"But you're not like that now. I can see that."

"I like to think that, but I'm not perfect," I finish off the beer, disappointed in myself. "It took my ex's husband, Jude, sitting my ass down years ago to talk some sense into me for Charlie's sake. I'm sorry to say that it doesn't always stick."

"You're a great father. I've seen how you and Charlie are together."

I scoff. "Far from it. I was just always on the road or

wasted whenever I did see her. Never even asked about her life."

Shame coils hot as flashes of Charlie's sad little face blurred through intoxicated hazes pierce my heart for the millionth time. "Missed a dance recital here, parent teacher conference there...the list is endless."

My voice sounds hollow. Haunted. As it probably should. "One birthday I was across the fucking country, but I promised her I'd make it back for her party." Bile burns my throat reliving the next morning's hungover realization I never even booked a fucking flight. Her crying eyes were red and swollen from tears when I Face-Timed with some shit excuse.

I meet Tess's empathy filled gaze. "I didn't even book the fucking trip back. What kind of asshole does that? Just thinks some gift in the mail or a fucking phone call erases all those times you shatter their freaking world."

I expel a harsh breath, regrets layering too deep to dive into completely tonight. But I need her to grasp the man I am, finally fighting his way free from his destructive roots.

She rubs my shoulder gently. "You're being too hard on yourself."

"Fuck. It's not even close to what I deserve." I meet her gaze, losing myself for a moment. "I was supposed to be the one convincing *you* I'm not an asshole, and somehow, you're now trying to convince *me*. I am damaged fucking goods, Tess. Fuck. Not even goods, just damaged."

"Well, I only know the Brad Chambers now. Not the

Brad Chambers of the past, so I can't exactly hold that against you." Her voice is kind, and it makes me bristle. I really don't deserve someone like her, and I fucking know it in my God damned soul.

"So, Gina didn't totally scare you off?" I ask, half afraid of the answer. And for some fucked up reason, I let hope spark to life inside of me. "If I were you, I'd be running for the fucking hills by now."

She's quiet for a moment, and my heart skips as I hold my breath. If this is it, at least I was fucking honest.

"No." She smiles, and it lights up the room. My whole world. "It will take a lot more than the likes of Gina to scare me off."

I let out the breath, and lift her hand to kiss her palm, holding it to my cheek. Fucking hell, my heart is racing.

"Thank you."

"So long as you're honest with me, there isn't much that could scare me."

"You might be able to survive this industry after all."

"Hey, I weathered and spun the sex scandal of Ohio's most popular senator. I can handle some rockstar exes." Her shoulders straighten with pride, and I can't help but sense a little fear still lingering under her bravado.

Mentally I promise myself to never give her a reason to doubt me again. She may put on a good front, but I know that deep down she's just like me, just like everyone else. We all have vulnerabilities and pain that we cover up for the sake of others.

I'll do everything I can to protect that.

sixteen
terrified

Tess

Am I fooling myself? Am I so attracted to this man that I'm putting blinders on to the truth of what a reality would look like with him? It's entirely possible, and lines up with my way of doing things. I like to think I'm a realist when it comes to my personal life, but I'm a dreamer, seeing things that I want to see. Believing things I have zero business believing.

I've been burned before by my own nature that way, and I can see that clearly happening here, but for some reason my instinct is kicking in. My heart is overruling my mind, blinding me to all the red flags, and I don't know exactly what to do with that. I should probably run away as fast as my feet can take me like he said, but there's something about Brad that won't let me do that.

I just hope that *something* doesn't come back to haunt me later down the road.

"So, date number one...Eventful," he chuckles, interlacing his fingers with mine. I love how our hands fit together so naturally.

"Definitely memorable," I say, smiling down at our hands.

"I guess that's not so bad, then, huh?"

"Not bad at all."

"Does that mean there will be a date number two?" he asks, and I love the hopefulness in his voice. Something about his tone melts away all the hesitation I've been experiencing the last few minutes. It makes me want to see where this goes even more.

"That would be nice."

"Nice?" he frowns. "We can do better than *nice...* can't we?"

My laughter echoes in the large practice space. "Great. That would be great. Fantastic, even. How's that?"

"Now we're talking." He leans over and kisses me gently. Just a brush of his lips whispering across mine. A chill skitters along my skin that is so delicious, I get goosebumps. "Let's shoot for the stars."

On the drive home, I find myself questioning everything. Brad. Gina. Myself. My entire life. Don't I know better than to think this will work out? Am I really thinking, 'What red flags?' It's as if I put rose-colored glasses on so I can't see them waving around because they're blending into the background. I'm overlooking them. On purpose.

Why do I do this to myself? What is so attractive about a man with a history like Brad's? Nothing. At least, of course, it's not his history that's attractive. It's him. Current him. I see how caring he is for Charlie. He's so good at making conversation and makes me laugh when I don't necessarily want to. And the way he looks at me sometimes, it's as if he sees right through to my soul. But is it just the idea of him that I like?

The potential?

I've been there, done that, when it comes to falling for someone's potential, only to have my heart stomped on when they don't live up to it. That's my own fault, though. The lost potential not meeting my invented expectations is never a fair fight. When I give that kind of responsibility for my emotions to someone else it never works. But isn't that part of a relationship too? You want to be with someone who makes you happy. Someone who you trust with your heart.

Can I trust Brad with mine?

I knew when I first met him that he was going to be trouble, and I was right. But is he the trouble? Or am I? Maybe I'm the problem. I'm overthinking this, like I do with everything.

A long sigh escapes me as I tighten my grip on the steering wheel. Tonight was just a small hiccup. It obviously wasn't planned that his ex-girlfriend would show up to spoil our date. But what Brad said about not knowing if it could happen again makes me worry. Sure, he's not his past, but it's something I'm going to have to fight with. Deal with. It's as if there are two of him: who he used to be, and who he is now. I'm not sure if I'm ready to deal with that, or if we can reconcile the two.

What's the old saying? *Two is company. Three is a crowd.*

When I get home, I run a hot bath, light some candles, and put on one of my old vinyl records. Comfort music. I need to clear my head, and this is one of my old standby ways to do it. Letting the heat relax my muscles, and the music relax my mind, all thoughts of Brad Chambers fade away for a minute.

But only for a minute because my phone dings with a text notification. I slowly open my eyes, instantly knowing who it's from, and my heart speeds up again. I can't help the butterflies battering around in my chest at the thought of him.

BRAD: Sorry again about tonight. I really did have a great time before...everything. But I am looking forward to date 2.

I hesitate before replying, searching my heart for what I really want to do now. My mind pictures the absolute sincerity in his eyes when he said he would die trying to convince me he's no longer a playboy. I believed him. My battered and tarnished heart believed him.

Am I really doing this?

I guess I am.

> ME: I had a great time too. Date 2 can only be better, right?

> BRAD: I like the way you think.
> Actually, I like everything about you.

Well, damn. I'm not sure how to respond to that, but he continues before I can.

> BRAD: Sorry. Sorry. Too much too
> soon. Jesus, I'm such a fuck up.

> ME: LOL. No worries. I like you too.

There's a long pause before either of us texts again, and now I'm afraid I went too far.

> BRAD: Cool. See you tomorrow.
> Sweet dreams.

> ME: Nite.

A warmth rushes through me, and it's not from the bath water. It's from Brad. Picturing him sitting at home, worried about my reaction to how our date ended does something to me. It endears me to him even further. Knowing that you're on someone's mind, even for just a moment, is a comfort. A safety. A small reassurance that your emotions are valid. *You* are valid.

For once in what feels like a *very* long time, I feel special.

Yup, I am totally doing this.

strange clouds

Brad

"Are you sure Dakota is going to be there today, Daddy?" Charlie asks for what feels like the millionth time from the back seat as we head to the practice space. I force back the eyeroll that wants to show itself and swallow the sarcastic comment that I was about to say.

I've got this fatherhood thing nailed down.

"Pretty sure, Pumpkin," I say, forcing a smile and some enthusiasm into my voice. Charlie's infatuation with our new bass player is a dynamic I don't know if I'm ready for. I doubt he's ready for it either. My smile turns genuine as I picture him trying to deal with my little girl's constant attention. Something he'll need to get used to.

There was something about Dakota during his audition that intrigued me. Sure, he gave off 'biggest fan' vibes at the start, but that faded as we all fell into step musically. He has this weird quietness about him that isn't typical in this world. Not necessarily an innocence;

quite the opposite. More like a hushed jadedness to him. A melancholy that runs deep. And I can't help but wonder what that's all about.

It's my nature to want to figure out what makes people tick, and I get the feeling that there is a lot more to Dakota than meets the eye. He's more than just a broody musician. There's a story there. The question is whether it's one he's willing to share.

As I pull into the studio parking lot, I push aside the negative thoughts remembering Gina popping up here last night, and see Dakota leaning against the building, beanie tugging low and a cigarette dangling from his lips. His lanky frame looks younger than his years, but that worn leather jacket and those combat boots tell another story. The contrast reminds me of myself not too long ago – world-wariness creeping into the edges of his youthful potential. I wonder when the light first began dimming behind those thoughtful eyes currently scanning something in a weathered notebook.

Charlie bounces out of the car, making a beeline for Dakota to resume her string of questions about his various punk accessories. A shy grin emerges beneath the dark hair at her bubbly attention. As much as Dakota's quiet calm contrasts our band's chaotic energy, having a soft spot for my daughter already earns him points around here.

Everyone deserves a chance to heal old scars with patience and care. If he sticks around, maybe Dakota will discover the found family all of us outcasts clung to during some difficult years. We're all just misfit toys embedding ourselves into each other's broken edges until the seams disappear. At least, that's what I tell myself.

I stride over to join them, determined to embrace Dakota into our world, one luminous brushstroke at a time to help restore whatever muted his colors.

Fuck, I'm in a poetic mood today. Is it Tess, that's got me pulling out the words today? I shouldn't question it. A muse is hard to find. Maybe I'll work on some lyrics today.

As I approach Dakota and Charlie, inspiration strikes me seeing this kindred spirit so cautiously opening up. My mind starts composing poetic phrases I can't wait to shape into raw lyrics. Dakota glances up, dark eyes unguarded for once without that innate wariness constantly shadowing each expression.

"She giving you the full inquisition yet on proper beanie care? She's apparently an expert," I joke easily. Dakota's shoulders relax while Charlie sticks her tongue out indignantly at me. I stick mine out right back.

"I tried explaining the intricate cleaning ritual I put it through, but think it got lost in translation..." Dakota replies wryly, a natural dynamic already emerging between us. Charlie's attention diverts suddenly to a vibrant bird flitting past.

I seize the opening as we head inside. "So, I gotta ask if you write songs at all too? Or are you mainly just a killer bass player?" Curiosity about his creative process prods me.

Dakota hitches his guitar case higher, glancing side-long. "I mess around sometimes, but generally keep my angsty ramblings to myself." He forces an offhand chuckle, but I recognize deflection way too easily.

"Well lucky for you angst makes kickass lyrics and I've got plenty of empty notebooks to fill..." I offer casually, hoping some sort of creative trust builds between us too in time. "Whenever you feel ready to pass some over..."

I clasp Dakota's shoulder supportively as we walk through the door framed by late morning light. Song lyrics have been tumbling around my brain like crazy the last few days, and I think I might have found my muse in Tess. But writing in Chaos Fuel is always a group effort, and I'm curious what Dakota might bring to the table. I have the feeling his creative well runs deep.

As we enter, I spot Tess sitting cross-legged on the studio's battered leather couch, tablet propped on her knees. Sunlight from the high windows sets her hair glowing like a golden halo, brow furrowed while she taps purposefully.

I halt, pulse instinctively rising a little just seeing her focused figure. Even in worn jeans with oversized headphones slipping down her slender neck, her elegance and beauty shines effortlessly. Dakota lifts his hand in an awkward wave before veering toward his gear stash. I barely notice, drinking in the graceful details of Tess I've sketched repeatedly in my brain.

She glances up, features easing from concentration into a breathtaking smile breaking across her face. My gut swoops helplessly, the way it does lately whenever her eyes catch mine. No matter how many moments like this we share, that thrill never goes away.

I walk over before my wandering mind composes sappy ballads right here and now. Perching on the couch arm, I stuff the love songs into a corner of my mind before they spill out. "So, how goes steering the social media love fest for our viral bass search winner?"

Tess lifts her headphones, sunlight haloing her in my artist's eye once more. "Well at least no one's threatened boycotting you guys over the beanie yet..."

Tess's teasing makes me grin as I watch her continue toggling photos on the tablet.

"Give it a day or two - the beanie fan club awaits," I volley back. Sobering, I add "For real though, think the fans will be cool with Dakota once his identity's out there?"

Tess smiles reassuringly. "If comments stay positive about the process like they have been so far, I'm hopeful." Her eyes trace fondly to where Dakota hunches over his guitar, lost in creative flow. "I think there's something deeper about him that will connect with fans."

My throat tightens at her insight being so on point without even trying. I nudge closer, craving more than surface banter now. "Even just doing PR, you can drop soulful truths without blinking..." I hesitate, unsure if such open admiration oversteps any of the guardrails we put in place.

Tess meets my eyes steadily and sets the tablet aside. Her palm presses gently over my restless fingers, the touch grounding my unsettled thoughts.

"Shining light where you want people to look isn't exactly groundbreaking or anything. But using something true when you do it at least gives it some sort of meaning." Her insight into how people work is fascinating at times. And it makes me wonder what the hell she sees in me.

"And where do you want people to look when it comes to me?" I ask, my curiosity overflowing now.

Her smile widens, and I can see a wave of answers roll through her. "I'm not sure yet."

"You're not sure?"

She diverts her gaze, her cheeks flushing slightly. "Well, I'm still getting to know you..."

"And...?"

"I don't like the idea of anyone else looking at you..."

That gets my heart racing, and I can feel my body electrify. So, she's the possessive type. Or at least the one-man type. I think I might like that. Actually, I'm positive that I do.

"Well, it is kind of my job," I tease, sliding closer, and resting my thigh against hers. The warmth of her body next to me is exhilarating. I want to be even closer.

"I know," she smiles, biting her lip and looking everywhere in the room except at me. It's fucking adorable. She's an absolutely horrible flirt, and it's even more attractive to me.

"So...when will date number two be?" I ask, leaning over and whispering the question in her ear. I can see her visibly shudder at my words, and a thrill runs through me that I have such an effect on her.

She finally glances over her shoulder at me, her suddenly shy eyes meeting mine. When they do, that electric current between us sparks to life again.

"I'm ready for it whenever you are."

Holy fucking shit. She's going to be the end of me, I know it. I can't with the sensuality that just oozes from her when she's not even fucking trying. How does she do that? Just a fucking look or a word from her and I'm completely undone.

"Let me find out when the next sleepover is..." I say immediately without thinking, and head over to where Ian is talking with Dakota. I'm on a fucking mission to schedule that sleepover for Charlie and make date two happen. And soon.

Whenever it happens, it won't be soon enough.

eighteen
sweet disposition

Tess

What has gotten into me? I've turned into some sort of feral cat in heat all of a sudden. I am not a flirt by any stretch of the imagination, but something about Brad just unravels me and my base instincts come out to play. From the looks of things, I don't think he minds at all, but I could be all kinds of wrong.

As he leaves to go talk to Ian, Charlie takes his spot next to me on the couch, a sober expression on her cute little face. Her red curls are up in a bouncy ponytail today, accentuating her young age.

"So, how was your date with my dad?" she asks, as if it's completely normal to talk about.

I am so thrown off kilter, I don't know how to respond at first. I don't want to get into details of anything that happened last night with Brad's daughter.

"It was great," I say, determined to keep things vague. This is a dynamic I didn't plan for when dating someone with a child. I knew it would be different but didn't anticipate this at all.

She eyes me skeptically, like a detective trying to solve an important case, and I'm the prime suspect evading justice.

"Just great?" she asks doubtfully, and I can tell she's seeing right through me. "Did you guys kiss?"

"Whoa, whoa, whoa," I say, raising my hands, trying to keep from blushing but failing miserably. "That's awfully personal, isn't it?"

Charlie shrugs noncommittally, as if personal questions are par for the course for her. I get the feeling they are. She might be too curious for her own good.

"Not really. I'm just curious." She eyes me suspiciously again, and I can feel myself squirm a little under the scrutiny.

"How old are you again?" I ask, trying to change the subject quickly.

"I'll be nine in a few months, but my dad says I'm going on thirty."

"I can see that," I nod. Wondering at her advanced maturity level. Is it because she's usually around adults? Or something else? I recall Brad's admission of being absent too much. That pain can age you faster than light.

"Are you going to go out again?" She's like a dog with a bone on this subject.

This, I can at least answer truthfully. "I hope so, yeah."

"Do you like him?"

There's something behind this question that hits

home with me. I can sense the history this little girl must have with Brad's exes making itself known somehow. My heart clenches at the thought of her getting attached, or hopeful, only to have her heart broken. She just wants consistency. Safety. Or maybe she just wants to see her dad happy. Either way, it endears me to her.

I know that feeling. That wishful thinking, and the hardness that comes with all the disappointment at such a young age. I can empathize with her, and know where this is all coming from, because I've lived it too.

"Yes," I sigh, resigned to sharing the truth. "I like him a lot."

Her gray eyes sparkle brightly, and I see a little bit of triumph there. Her matchmaking is bearing fruit. For now, anyway. I really don't want to be another disappointment for her, but that added pressure isn't one I've prepared for.

Three's a crowd?

No. Not with Charlie. She and Brad count as one. They are a package deal, and I'm perfectly okay with that. I really like Charlie. Her personality isn't typical for her age, and I love that about her. She's special. And I'll do everything I can to make sure that never changes.

Later in the day, we're all taking a break from the rehearsals, scattered around the room doing our own thing for a few minutes. I catch Brad on the couch with Charlie on his lap while he reads a book to her. It's such a tender moment, I instinctively grab my phone for a photo, but end up recording a video of the two of them instead.

The sweetness between them does something to my heart, and a lightbulb goes off in my head. *This* is the spotlight he needs. This is what will fix whatever seems broken with the fans. They need to see this side of Brad. The soft side. The tender side. The side that isn't partying, or womanizing, or whatever negative things they think about him.

This is the Real Brad.

Before I can second guess myself, I post the video to all of Chaos Fuel's social media accounts. Within seconds, the positive responses start pouring in.

Bullseye.

Nailed it.

Some days I love my job. Especially when something random and out of the blue works and strikes the right chord. Like this. Social media wins are hard to come by...

And I just hit a freaking home run.

nineteen
say it

Brad

Reading a chapter to my girl from her favorite book, *The Worst Witch*, during a break in rehearsals is a nice switch for my brain. I've been in a heightened mode of creativity for hours straight, so to relax for a minute and decompress with someone else's words for a change feels good. I love that Charlie still likes this book too after reading it so many times.

Things like this book are an odd comfort. Predictability gives a sense of safety when everything else around is overwhelming. Knowing how something is going to go in a story can calm a racing heart or whirring mind. It's that security that we're all searching for in some way, and why we rewatch certain shows or movies, or listen to the same song over and over.

Repetitiveness is reinforcing the emotion we've pulled from it. We need something from it. Crave it. Hunger for it. And I see why we do it. There is nothing wrong with wanting to find comfort. I can only hope that people find comfort in our music in the same way. It's kind of why we do it.

To relate.

To connect.

I catch Tess's eye when I glance up for a second, and find her watching us, a faraway look in her gaze. It's as if she's somewhere else, or at least seeing or thinking about somewhere or something else. It gives her a dreamy look that is fascinating to me. My heart pounds briefly, hoping that it's me she's thinking about with that look on her face. I want her daydreaming about me, like I've been fighting against all morning with her only feet away from us while we practice.

I can't explain the magnetic pull of her. Sure, she's hot as fuck, and super smart and funny, but it's something else. Something more. I'm dying to find out what that something more could be.

According to Ian, the girls can have another sleepover this Friday, so fingers crossed that date number two with Tess goes smoothly this time. I'm not going to put pressure or expectations on anything, but I'd be a fucking liar if I didn't say I want to take things to the next level with her. Whether or not we get there is yet to be seen, but I'm willing to go wherever she leads us.

I finish reading the chapter and Charlie hops off my lap and runs to join Hayley and June in the craft corner. She's been antsy to join them for a few minutes now, so I'm happy to put her out of her misery. Besides, my eyes are getting tired.

Tess comes to sit next to me, and it takes about all I

have in me not to wrap an arm around her, or reach out and touch her hair, or her cheek. Run a thumb along her bottom lip as she breathes in. Fuck, kiss her right here and now in front of everyone.

Somehow, I restrain myself.

She gives me a sideways glance as if she knows exactly what ran through my mind, and we share a smile between us. A secret smile. One that conveys the emotions running through both of us. I hate secrets, but this one I don't mind keeping. For now, at least.

"So, what have you been up to, slaving over your phone the last half hour or so?" I ask, curious what that faraway look was in her eyes not long ago. "Or were you just listening to me read out loud?"

She smirks, and I love it. "I was listening, yes, but I was also working..." The smirk turns into a wide smile as she holds her phone out for me to look at.

It's a video of me reading to Charlie, and to be honest, it's fucking amazing. The lighting, the setting, it perfectly shows my relationship with Charlie.

"Wow. That's really cool...can you send me a copy of that? I'd love to have it for myself." It's one of those videos I could show Charlie later, when she's going through her teenage angst and say, *'See, we used to be cool.'*

"Oh, I guess I could send it," she says, a little awkwardly. "But I put it up on all your socials, so you have it there already. The response has been great—"

My bones freeze.

"You did what??" I pray to God I didn't just hear

what I think I heard. Using Charlie in any way is out of the fucking question.

"I put it on your socials to show a different side of you..." Tess's eyes are growing wide and surprised at my sharp response.

"Tess, no. Absolutely not."

"But the response has been great. Everyone loves it."

"Give me that," I snap, grabbing her phone to read the comments that I'm sure aren't going to be so positive. I know how fucking cruel the internet is.

And I'm fucking right.

angryboi69: Man, he's fucking 'em younger and younger now, huh? Scum.

freesprite: At least we know he can read now.

imthatguy: a few more years, I'd do her.

My hands are shaking, I'm so fucking irate.

"Take it down now," I seethe through gritted teeth. "Fucking NOW, Tess."

Her brow furrows in confusion as she takes the phone away from me and starts scrolling the comments.

"Oh my God," she mumbles, her own hands starting to tremble as she reads. She starts hurriedly tapping the screen and flipping between apps, hopefully deleting the post from everywhere she uploaded it. "Oh my God, I'm so sorry. I am so, so sorry."

The damage is done, however, and I can't even begin to mentally deal with the aftermath of this, whatever it's going to look like. What the hell made Tess think posting a video of my daughter online was a good idea? Or to do it without asking first?

I get up to take Charlie home early. I need to get the fuck out of here and take my girl with me. My protective instincts are flying into place and taking over. Just as I'm about to head over to her, my phone starts ringing. Glancing down, I see that it's Ren, Charlie's mom.

Fuck.

Fuck.

We're in for it now.

twenty
blurry

Tess

Oh, my God. What have I done?

How did I not think that post through? Not realize that the world of full of monsters with smart phones ready and willing to ruin anything decent. I know better. Hell, my *job* is to know better, and I just fucked it up in the grandest way possible.

As soon as Brad questioned it, I knew I'd misstepped. I was so caught up in his moment with Charlie, and filled with an emotion so wholesome and endearing, that I wanted to share it with the world. I wanted to show the universe what a great guy he truly is, what a wonderful dad he can be outside of the spotlight, how loving and patient he is with his daughter. I wanted to shout it from the rooftops.

But that was my mistake.

I made it personal. To *me*. And I know better than to let my personal feelings mix with my work. At least, I should. I've been at this long enough to know how this goes, what the reaction would be, what kind of nasty comments all posts get. I should have protected Charlie from that. I should have protected both of them.

I *should* have taken a beat before posting.

All regret is full of *'could've, would've, should've,'* and mine is no different. It's eating away at me as I watch Brad hang up his phone angrily and gather up Charlie to take her home early. She's a little confused, at first, at the sudden change in schedule, but happily concedes after promises of ice cream.

"Is Tess coming with us?" she asks, innocently looking my way as they head toward the exit. The hopefulness in her eyes cuts into my soul. That disappointment I wanted to keep away from her is about to hit her head on, and I feel sick to my stomach knowing I'm the cause of it.

This isn't how things are supposed to go.

"No," Brad says sharply, his lips drawn in a flat line as he avoids my gaze while they walk. "She's not."

The finality of his words hurt. Deeply.

More than I expected them to.

And I can see the crash happen as it hits Charlie, but I can't look away. It's like watching a car accident in slow motion as her little brows furrow at her father's tone and words. She's trying desperately to adjust to the sudden shift in mood in the room and looking to me for answers.

I have none.

I have nothing.

I manage to force a weak smile on my face and wave to her as they rush out the door. The silence that falls over the room once they're gone is heavy, and I look around to see everyone's eyes on me. Questioning.

Rehearsal is apparently over.

How they know that Brad's quick exit is my fault, I have no idea, but I have no words to offer anyone. I'm still processing everything that's happened in the last five minutes, and it's a jumbled mess.

In the matter of a heartbeat, I made a horrible professional judgment call, carved a gaping divide between myself and someone I was starting to really care about, and disappointed an innocent little girl. And, who the fuck knows what the repercussions are going to be for the band? This could go all kinds of sideways.

Posting and deleting things so quickly actually gets noticed more than something that gets left up. This is going to be so bad. I can't even fathom how horribly this is going to resonate with the fan base.

I don't get time to start sorting anything out in my brain as my phone starts vibrating in my hand. I glance down and see that it's Eliza from Blackmore. She's probably wondering what the hell just happened online too.

My heart skips, and then starts racing. *This is where I get fired...*

Glancing up, but not meeting anyone's eyes, I move to head outside to take the call. "Excuse me," I mutter, nearly tripping over a cord in my hurry to escape their curious stares.

When I push through the door to the parking lot, I catch Brad's car pulling onto the street, the sunlight glinting off the rear window. My impulse is to chase after them. Flag him down to apologize, but I'm paralyzed with guilt on the spot.

I'm unable to see him or Charlie, but I can picture their faces; Brad, trying to stifle his anger, and Charlie trying to wrap her head around what's going on. She's a smart girl. She knows something is up.

How I wish I could explain it to her. Like I probably have to explain it to Eliza now.

I accept the call right before it goes to voicemail.

"Hey, Eliza. What's up?" I ask, trying hard to switch into professional mode, and leave my emotions behind. It's impossible, though, since everything is bubbling up to the surface. I swallow hard, preparing myself for the onslaught about to overtake me.

"You tell me," she says matter-of-factly. I normally love that Eliza is all business, but right now it's scaring me to death. "What just happened with the socials for Chaos Fuel? I just heard something was posted and then deleted?"

I don't answer right away, trying to pull myself and an answer together at the same time. I need to navigate this carefully, no matter how reckless my heart is feeling now.

"Tess?" she prods.

Taking a deep breath, I swallow hard. "I'm here," I start, knowing that the truth is the only play here. "I mistakenly posted a video of Brad and his daughter, thinking it was a good idea to show a softer side of him. Unfortunately, I didn't think it through completely." I pause, my heart wrenching. "I also didn't get permission to use Charlie beforehand like I should have."

It's Eliza's turn to be quiet, and her silence is deafening. I can only imagine the ways she's picturing firing me right here and now. This is a major fuck up. One that someone in my position should know better than commit. We both know it.

I start pacing and chewing on a nail, balancing nervously on the curb of the walkway to distract myself. The longer the silence stretches, the more nervous I get.

All I can do is explain myself. There is no defense.

"Once I realized my mistake, I took it down everywhere. But obviously the damage is already done," I say, feeling small and defeated.

"I see," is all she says, letting the words hit. And they do. Right in the heart. The disappointment in those two words just compounds with my own, and I feel like I'm drowning. The surface where all the air is grows further out of my reach.

"Really, Eliza. I don't normally make mistakes like this. I got caught up in the moment, and thought it was something to bridge the gap with the fans. And the initial response was exactly as I'd hoped...but then..." I drift off, not wanting to remember all the vile comments that started pouring in.

"Then people happened," she sighs.

"Well, people...and Brad." I wince, picturing the protective anger in his beautiful features directed at me. "He was especially not happy."

"Rightfully so."

"Exactly," I agree. "He has every right to be mad at me right now. It was a horrible idea. I shouldn't have posted that without his permission."

My stomach twists into knots as I internalize everything. Every negative emotion hurled my way right now is deserved, and I know it. Using a child to sway public opinion is the lowest of the low, and I can't believe I did it.

Me – a so-called professional.

I nearly teeter off the curb I'm balancing on when Eliza says, "Here's the thing – it worked."

My pacing stops abruptly. "What? What worked?"

There's a sly smile in her voice that I was not prepared for. "You haven't checked the aftermath, have you?"

"No...?" I've barely had time to register what I did, let alone look to see what's being said about it. It's been a whopping twenty minutes since I deleted the post. If that.

"It's still early, obviously, but people are already posting screen grabs with reaction videos, raving about seeing an intimate side of Brad. It's struck a chord with the fans."

My emotions crash into each other violently at this news. Part of me feels triumphant that my initial instinct was correct, but another part – the larger part, hates how it came about. How I betrayed an unspoken trust with Brad to protect his daughter. I hate that any success might come out of me fucking up so badly.

"I see," I say flatly, repeating Eliza's words back to

her. I really can't think of anything else to say. I can't say, "Good," because it's not. It's not good at all. In fact, it's downright horrible. There are now echoes of my mistake floating around the internet.

It's now eternal. Immortal. It's never going to end.

As fast as this conversation with Eliza came to be, it only proves the point that anything posted on the internet is forever. I'll never be able to escape this now.

And neither will Charlie. Or Brad.

"Look, most people say this about God, but the internet truly works in mysterious ways," Eliza says, interrupting my self-destructive thoughts.

"But Brad—"

"Will get over it." Her confidence in her words is so magnetic, I almost believe them.

"I'm not so sure about that, Eliza," I say, knowing in my heart there's more truth in my words than hers. Plus, I'm supposed to be a social media expert. I *do* know how these things work. Brad and Charlie will now have to deal with this for a long time to come. "You didn't see him leave just now."

She sighs thoughtfully before saying, "I've worked with a lot of musicians. Hell, I even married a couple of them. I know how they tick. They're all emotions. But here's the thing, those emotions change. Frequently. They're ready to punch walls one minute, and reciting poetry the next. It's whiplash in its finest form. You just need to be able to navigate it and hang on for the ride. Trust me, he will get over it."

I feel the truth in her words, as I've seen it myself

with Brad on our date. The switch in his emotions when Gina showed up and then back again was dizzying but is also part of what attracts me to him. Is that normal?

This situation is totally different.

"But this is about his daughter, Eliza," I say, cringing inwardly at my own shame. "He's not going to get over that."

"Let me talk to him," she says after a pause.

"Wait. So, I'm not fired?" I ask, my brain still playing catch up to this entire conversation, let alone the situation itself.

"Of course not," she says, matter-of-factly. As if the thought is the stupidest one in the world. "While the route you took is questionable, the results speak for themselves. I can't deny that. And neither can Brad once he looks at it more closely."

I'm only partially relieved to still have a job. Mostly, I'm still roiling with guilt at my mistake. Not only did I cross an ethical line, but I broke the trust I was building with Brad. The relationship we were building now lays in ashes at my feet. That's more important than any job. That hurts the most.

While Eliza can most likely patch over whatever professional bridges have been burned between me and Brad, I'll never be able to repair the personal ones. Any thought of something sparking between the two of us is now doused completely.

I've ruined it.

I've ruined everything.

twenty-one
be yourself

Brad

T he entire ride home was excruciating, with Charlie
lobbing questions at me like it's an Olympic
sport, and she's going for the gold medal. I can only
deflect so much since she's so fucking smart. She knows
something is going on, and from her questions, she has
an idea that it has to do with Tess.

Fuck me.

It's hard enough to deal with my own thoughts and
feelings in this, but I also have to contend with Ren and
Jude breathing down my neck from across the world.
Today, I am not a fan of technology. How quickly Ren
knew about the post, saw the post, and then called to
bitch at me about it is mind boggling. It had to have been
only a matter of minutes from going up or coming down
for her to react so fast.

But I also can't blame her for her reaction since it
mirrored mine. Charlie is off limits to any outsiders,
including press and social media. As parents who happen

to be in the limelight, we agreed on that years ago. Of course, back then, it was more because she was married to Jude Lockwood of Indigo King. My spotlight is recent, but that doesn't make it any less glaring when it comes to my daughter.

To be fair, Tess and I never discussed the boundaries regarding Charlie in that way, but I don't feel like fighting fair right now. No, I want to rage because I still feel betrayed. It's not even what she posted, because, yeah, it was a fucking great video of me and Charlie. I actually love the video. Or at least I did.

But she didn't fucking ask.

She just took it upon herself to post a video of my little girl to social media for all the troll piranhas to eat her alive. Not a single fucking thought of what that means to me or her mother, or to fucking Charlie herself. Yes, she took it down, but God only knows how many assholes captured it somehow to use in ways I don't even want to imagine.

My blood curdles at the horrendous thoughts running through my mind. *People are sick fucks.*

"Daddy, can I have some ice cream?" Charlie's voice cuts through my downward mental spiral.

I need to blink a few times to bring her into focus. "Sure thing, baby girl," I say, standing from the couch I just fell onto and rolling my shoulders, trying to release the tension building up inside of me.

"I'm not a baby," she whines, *just like a baby*, as she trails after me into the kitchen.

"Yeah, well, you're *my* baby, and always will be.

Don't you forget it." I grab some bowls from the cupboard and start scooping the ice cream for both of us. "You'll be thirty-five, married to some dude with a desk job and a tie, with your own hoard of rugrats, and you'll still be my baby girl. Got it?"

She giggles as she scrunches her nose at me. "Eww. A tie? Really?"

I stop and stare at her, playing up the disbelief. "What? You don't like ties?"

She shakes her head at me, still smirking. "Nope."

"Oh, that's right. You like beanies." I smack my forehead. "I totally forgot about that."

Her cheeks flush almost as red as her hair, but she snatches one of the bowls of ice cream and a spoon from the counter and rushes to the living room without another word. That'll keep her quiet for a few minutes at least.

As much as I love teasing her about shit like that, something in my gut twists at the thought of little Charlie eventually dating. If I'm honest with myself, that time is going to come a lot quicker than I want it to. I am not going to handle that well at all. Especially if this video incident is any fucking indication. I'm going to have to lock her in a tower or something, like in one of those Disney movies we enjoy trash-talking together.

If only.

After a few hours of dealing with Charlie's sugar rush and subsequent crash, there's a knock on the apartment door. I haven't looked at my phone this whole time because I don't want to see any of the fallout. Not yet. I'll deal with it once Charlie goes to bed and I can focus my attention on it. Not to say it hasn't been in the back of my mind, because it has been. A lot.

My first instinct and thought are that it's Tess. She somehow got my address and is here to apologize. My adrenaline pumps up a little, a small flicker of hope rushing through me that we can put this all behind us. But then I remember what she did, and that hope fizzles. I can't *want* to work things out. So why the fuck do I all of a sudden?

"Dad?" Charlie asks, her brow creased with concern.

I snap out of it and look at her. "What's up?"

"Are you going to see who it is?" The arch in her brow is bordering on sarcasm, and it dawns on me that I haven't moved. I've been lost in my head.

Again. *Fuck.*

The knock on the door repeats, and it's a little louder this time. Reluctantly, I get up and head to answer the door.

When I open it, I find Dakota on the doorstep. Not Tess. The disappointment that rolls through me makes zero sense, but I shove it down, and plaster on a smile.

"Hey, man. What's up?" I say, offering a hand for an awkward handshake that turns into something like a bro-ritual. First a regular handshake, that morphs into an arm-wrestling pose, then another position that feels weird. After a few transitions I give up and drop my hand, feeling like an idiot who doesn't know the first thing about 'cool bro' handshakes.

Fair enough.

Dakota is unphased, but still seems a bit reserved. His beanie is missing, and his hair is tied back low on the nape of his neck. Charlie will be so disappointed.

"I wasn't sure if I should still show up for our lyric session," he starts, still in the doorway, glancing around the living room, "since you guys left so early... I tried texting, but thought I'd swing by anyway in case I had your number wrong."

Holy shit. I totally forgot we planned this earlier today. In all that's happened since this afternoon, it completely slipped my mind that I'd invited Dakota over to write together.

"Sorry about that, dude, come on in. It's all good." I force a smile as Charlie runs over to greet Dakota. Maybe she's not so disappointed after all.

Girls.

It takes a good half hour to convince Charlie that she needs to get ready for bed. She's wrapped up in all things Dakota, tossing a million questions at him, and he's wrapped around her little finger. Just where she wants him.

At least I have company.

When she finally concedes and goes to her room, I head into the kitchen. "Can I get you a beer or something?"

Dakota follows me in, leaning his lanky frame against a counter. "Nah, I'm good. I don't drink."

I pause for a minute, holding the fridge door open and glance over to study him. It's almost unheard of to not drink in the music business. But then it's usually one extreme or another. People either party too much, or not at all. There isn't a lot of gray area.

It makes me wonder even more what Dakota's story is. "You don't? Which is it? Can't? Won't? or don't?"

"Yes."

"That's valid," I say, seeing that he doesn't want to get into it, and I'm not one to press anything now. I've got my own shit. "Water, then?"

"That'd be great." He loosens up a little at my not prying for further details, as if he was expecting to get the third degree from me.

We settle on the couch and start going through his notebooks, which is more like poetry than lyrics. The guy has a gift with words, and it makes me start to question my own talent as a songwriter. I'm no Shakespeare, but Dakota's writing resonates on a deeper level. A level that I'm not usually willing to go to in a song.

I'm all for pouring my heart and soul into a song, but I seem to stop myself before it gets too close to home. I go to the heart of it, but not *my* heart. My defenses won't let me expose that to anyone, not really.

But Dakota's writing is almost *too* personal. One part captures my attention:

The void we hid in took you.

Back to the reality we ran from,
Stolen, or stupid, either way successful
In losing you forever
To The Abyss.

I read the entire thing a few times, and let the emotion of it sink in. The grief and longing in the words wash over me and strike a chord that I can relate to. Especially today.

"This is good stuff, man," I say quietly. He's been picking at the loose threads on his ripped jeans as I read, and I can sense his discomfort. It's not easy to share your soul like this. I get it.

He lifts his shoulder slightly in response, not meeting my eyes, or saying a word. It's almost painful to watch.

But curiosity is killing me. I need to know what this is about.

"Can you give me some context to this?" I ask, still treading carefully. I really don't know Dakota at all, and this feels like an important moment. "If you can, I mean. I don't want to pry into your personal shit."

He shakes his head slowly, obviously considering whether to spill his secrets or not. I can relate.

"It...was about my wife," he finally says, his voice barely a whisper. His face is stoic, but his eyes are deeply haunted.

"You're married?" I can't hide the surprise in my voice. I think he's around twenty-six or seven, but he still seems too young to be married for some reason. There's a quiet innocence about him that I think I project on to him since he was originally just a fan. But now that I look closer, I can see that any age about him comes from experience.

"I was..." he starts, hesitating and looking away. The ghosts in his gaze brightening. "She died two years ago."

Fuck.

"Shit, man. I'm sorry. I didn't mean to get so personal." The pieces start clicking into place in my brain. The lyrics. The haunted expression. The not partying. The story. It all makes sense now. And it puts a lot of shit into perspective for me.

He waves me off. "Nah, no worries, dude. It's cool."

It's a standard brush off, and I recognize it, because I do it too. We all do. Saying things are 'cool' when they're not. I can clearly see in everything about him that his late wife's death still affects him deeply.

I brave another question, wanting to know all he's able to tell me. "Can I ask how she died?"

He leans forward then, resting his elbows on his knees as he plays with the wrap-around snake ring on his ring finger, his head lowered. It's then that I notice a line tattoo underneath the snake. The old wedding band tattoo that was popular a few years ago. My heart wrenches at the sight of it.

"You don't have to go into it if you don't want to, man," I clarify, not wanting to make him any more uncomfortable than he obviously already is. We don't know each other well enough yet for all our life stories to be told.

"She OD'd," he says bluntly, and there's an edge of animosity in his tone, or maybe it's plain old anger. That's fair.

Click.

So, I was right, at least. Everything added up to that, but I didn't want to assume anything.

"I'm sorry."

He shrugs again, but stays silent, still twirling the ring around his finger.

There are moments when people share things when words just won't cut it. Or too many words will diminish it somehow. This is one of those. He doesn't need a long diatribe about how much his situation sucks. He knows it already. He also doesn't need a monologue from me about any of my own experiences with people who have OD'd. They don't matter to him. I don't matter in this situation.

It's *his* situation.

All I can do is keep it short. To the point. *I'm sorry.*

Sometimes that's all a person needs to hear – that someone is sorry that they've had to go through something. They don't want the full-blown pity party, just the greeting card. Just a few words to make them feel seen.

And, man, do I see him right now.

Not that I've lost a significant other to drugs, but I've lost people. Friends. It's an unfortunate side to this industry, hell, to life in general. It happens.

Shit happens.

I feel a bit hardened to it at times, but shit like this, like Dakota's story, softens me back to it. His lyrics give it all meaning again.

"Would you mind if we used these?" I pick the notebook back up and point to the page in question. "In a song, I mean."

The hesitation is back, and I can see his mind running a million miles an hour behind his hazel eyes.

Eventually, he nods. And it's not just a half-hearted nod, it's emphatic.

"Yeah, I wish you would, actually."

It's an odd response, and one I wasn't expecting to say the least. I thought he'd fight it just a little bit more, but I'm glad to hear it.

"Did you already have a melody in mind? Or some sort of structure?" I get up from the couch and grab my old acoustic guitar from a nearby stand, anxious to see where this could go.

"I did, actually," he says, brightening a little as he takes the guitar from me and starts playing.

He is not a singer, by any stretch of the imagination, but I get the gist of the melody he had in mind and start singing along as he plays. The contrast between the melody and the notes played gives it an even more haunting aura, and after about another hour of working and reworking, I think we have a song on our hands.

Pain can be powerful.

twenty-two
still here

Tess

After going over the online situation with Ian once Brad left, I drag myself to meet Ivy for dinner. Honestly, I'd rather just go home and bury myself under a rock or something, but she insisted I come and talk about what happened.

"So, you fucked up," Ivy says. A declaration that I now need to contextualize for her. She's so good at pulling stories out of me that I don't want to tell. I hate her for it, and love that she can do it at the same time.

"I did," I agree, and spill the entire thing. One thing about Ivy is that she'll get all the details eventually, so I just throw them out there to begin with. It saves time in the long run.

Once I finish spilling my guts about the whole ordeal and the conversation with Eliza, she twists her wine glass by the stem thoughtfully for several minutes, obviously lost in thought. It makes me uncomfortable, but I wait her out. Surely she's got some pearls of wisdom to share with me to make it all better. At least, I really hope she does.

Finally, she nods to herself and locks my gaze with hers. "You care about him a lot already, don't you?"

I tilt my head at her, a little confused at the question. "I guess, but—"

"That's not an answer," she interrupts. "Yes, or no? You really like Brad Chambers?"

I take a sip of my own wine, searching for my feelings. I can't deny them. Not with Ivy. And a part of me dies a little at the thought that I've screwed it all up so badly. "I do. Yeah."

She nods to herself again, still studying me. "Then you need to fix this."

I roll my eyes, getting frustrated. That's not an answer. I need a solution. "No shit. But, how?"

"Here's the thing," she says, leaning forward on the table, her voice low. Her soulful eyes are full of empathy. "Brad is a father of a little girl. A very protective father from the sound of things. You may not have known that a line was there when it came to Charlie, but you crossed it."

"I know..."

"All you can do is be honest with him. Own up to your mistake and hope he can get past it."

It's not the grand scheme I was hoping for to instantly fix everything, but she's right. I'm not a schemer anyway. Even if she did come up with some spectacular plot, I'd fuck it up if it wasn't based in truth somehow.

"And, what if he can't? What if I've ruined things beyond repair?" My throat tightens as I ask the question, because I don't want that to be the case. I want to fix this.

"That's a question for you," she replies, tilting her wine glass toward me. "What are you going to do if he can't? Can you still work for the band if there's a tension there between you and Brad? Would you want to?"

I consider the question. Of course, I *could* still work with the band, but would I want to? I don't think I would. Seeing Brad as a daily reminder of what could have been would be too much for my sensitive soul. Seeing him with someone else eventually would be even worse. I don't think I could handle that.

But aren't I a professional? Sure, this situation puts that all into question, but the reality of the situation is that I am. I should be able to put my emotions aside to do my job. I do that all the time for clients. Why is this so different?

Because I really do like Brad. A lot. More than I should? I don't know how to navigate this until I know what Brad is thinking.

"Technically, I think I could still work for them, but I don't think I'd want to." I pause, letting the possibility sink in. "It would hurt too much."

"Then talk to him," Ivy says, "You've been through enough shit with losers with the broken trust reversed. Use that. You know what he's going through, what he's feeling. You've been there. Not exactly like this, but you know what I'm saying."

She's right. Of course she's right. I do know what it's

like to have trust broken, because it happens to me *all the time*. I've just never been on this side of it before. I don't like it.

"I do know what you're saying. And you're right. I'm just not used to being the trust breaker. I'm usually the one being fucked over, remember?"

"To be fair, though, this was unintentional, so don't beat yourself up too much. It was an honest mistake." She snickers. "It's not like you 'accidentally' fell into someone else's bed... I will not be naming names."

She doesn't have to. I know exactly who she's referring to. Unfortunately, it's more than one of my ex-boyfriends who have 'accidentally' or otherwise 'mistakenly' fucked someone else while still in a relationship with me.

I sure can pick 'em.

"Please don't," I say, trying to take her words to heart. I didn't mean to break Brad's trust, she's right.

I just need to convince him of that. Somehow.

When I get home, I pace. A lot. I silently wish that I had a pet of some kind to comfort me, or hell, even pace the floor with me. With all the traveling I've done in previous jobs, it never felt prudent to keep a pet. Shit, I'd even settle for a short-lived carnival goldfish right now just for the company.

I already apologized to Brad at the rehearsal space, so I don't want to beat a dead horse with the 'I'm sorry's,' but I can't help wanting to say it again, over, and over. I'll say it until I'm blue in the face if it means he believes me. And forgives me.

That's the part that pulls at me. I need him to forgive me. With every fiber of my being, I want him to tell me that it's going to be alright. We can get past this. We can continue from where we left off before I screwed it all up.

I need to know that it's not unfixable.

After too many trips around the living room, I finally brace myself and dial his number. It's late, but not that late. Not for Brad. I know he's a night owl like me, so as the phone rings without an answer, I hold my breath.

After the fourth ring, his voice is breathy, but with an edge to it that sets my nerves into a frenzy.

"Hello."

It's not a question. Or a greeting. Just a word. And I don't know how to interpret it. There is no emotion at all.

"I was hoping we could talk," I say, pushing through my anxiety and trying desperately to not be too tentative. I'm calling with a purpose, and I want him to know that.

"Okay."

That short response isn't exactly encouraging, but I press forward.

"I've already apologized, so I'm not going to keep telling you how sorry I am," I start, but then the wind in my sails starts to wane. Maybe that's not the best way to start this. "But I hope you know that I *am* sorry."

Nothing. Not even a sigh. Damnit, though, this is too important.

"What I wanted to talk about were my intentions. Because I never, *ever*, intended to cross any sort of line with you. Or Charlie. I absolutely one hundred percent should have asked you before posting that video."

"We agree on that," he says flatly.

"Brad, in one week I've seen sides of you that the public never sees. And it kills me to think that people are out there that don't know how wonderful of a human being you are. That don't know what a fantastic father you are. And when I saw you with Charlie, reading like that, I wanted people to see that side of you. I just didn't stop to think, and I should have. I let my personal feelings for you cloud my professional judgment."

He's quiet for a long moment, and for a second, I think maybe he's hung up on me. But then he says, "Charlie really likes you, Tess. And I'll be honest, that scares me. Especially after today."

My heart cracks, remembering Charlie's confused face as they left earlier. I never meant to do this to her either.

"Well, I really like her, too. And I feel like absolute shit."

Now we're both quiet, and I can almost hear both of our minds whirring with indecision.

I break the silence, resigned to resolve this one way or the other. "Listen, I spoke with Eliza earlier, and I'm not fired, but if you're uncomfortable working with me, just say the word, and I'll quit tomorrow—"

"No, I don't want you to quit your job..." he sighs. "Fuck, I don't even think I want to stop seeing you. But I need you to understand that Charlie is off limits on all things Chaos Fuel related."

My heart jumps as I try to digest what he's just said. "So, wait. You forgive me?"

He laughs softly, and it's music to my ears. "Yes, Tess. I forgive you. I know it wasn't intentional. It's just--" His voice turns serious, but I can still hear the smile. "Just please don't do it again."

While he seems to be making light of everything now for my benefit, I know deep down that he's serious, and I understand. I also know that I'll never make this kind of mistake again.

Ever.

But I can't help feeling that it's not completely resolved between us. I'm going to have to earn his trust back somehow.

Am I up to the task?

twenty-three
chokehold

Brad

Forgiveness. It's such a weird fucking word. Sure, whatever fucked up thing you did is now totally fine. How does somebody get to that point of acceptance? Like, completely? Is it even possible? Or is forgiveness just for your own peace of mind? It's just to let something go that hurts you. Either way, it feels difficult as fuck.

Do I want to forgive Tess? Absolutely. I know deep down that her mistake was unintentional. I know that in my soul. I may not know Tess that well, but I do at least know that about her. She wouldn't purposely do something to harm Charlie, or me. Or anyone, really. That's just not her.

So, why do I have a nagging thought in the back of my mind to be careful now? When just yesterday I was willingly throwing myself at her? Ready to jump feet first into the deep end of whatever it is we're doing with each other. Suddenly, my feet are a little on the chilly side, and I'm not sure what to do with that.

"Let's just take it day by day and see what happens," I offer, not quite ready to commit to anything solid. It feels like the ground is shifting beneath me, and I want to get a little steadier before moving forward.

I can tell by Tess's response that she's not happy with my suggestion.

"Okay..." Her voice sounds small, and I hate the sound of it.

"I just need the dust from this to settle," I say, not wanting to cast any more shadows on this relationship. It's already been a rocky start. "You know? We don't seem to make anything easy on ourselves, do we?"

There's a bit of a sigh and laugh on the other end of the line, and I can picture Tess's smile shining through her nervousness. Something about it pulls at me. Maybe after the emotional evening with Dakota, some internal doors were left open.

"No," she breathes out. "But then nothing worthwhile ever comes easy, right?"

"Well, that's bullshit. Life needs to stop with all the complications already. It's hard enough as it is." I consider Dakota again, and the grief that seems to still emanate from him when he thinks no one is looking. "Sometimes we just need a fucking break from having to try so hard just to survive."

"That's fair," Tess says. "It would be nice for things to be easy for a change. I don't know if I'd know how to react if they were, though."

"I get that. Like if it's easy, it's *too* easy. It's suspicious to not have something wrong."

"Well, I guess we don't have to worry about that problem anymore." I can't tell if she's joking, but she's not wrong. Today did complicate things. And I'm not sure exactly how I feel about the whole thing.

An alarm has been raised somewhere in my head, but my heart is still in this. I think. The two need to get their shit together and agree already.

I only hope this feeling is temporary.

When we get to the practice space the next day, any and all doubts I had about Tess get thrown out the fucking window. As soon as I see her, everything I like about her overtakes me. From how her smile grows wide when Charlie runs over to her, a real smile that lights up the room, to the trepidation in her eyes when she looks at me. She's nervous that I'm still mad at her, and from the moment her eyes meet mine, any anger I may have been holding onto dissipates into the ether.

There's no avoiding it. I like Tess.

My return smile is just as genuine, and she must sense that I've let things go as her shoulders relax ever so slightly. There's a pang of guilt that I made her feel tense in any way, but I shove it aside. I was only protecting my daughter. There's no shame in that.

I had time overnight and this morning to look at the full picture. It's all about intentions for me. If you don't intend to hurt someone with your actions, that needs to be taken into consideration when dealing with the fall-out. I know deep down that Tess never intended to harm us. Her reactions were instant, remorseful, and loud and clear.

I also know first-hand that people make mistakes because I'm usually the one making them. It's been my modus operandi for as long as I can remember. And if people, including Charlie, didn't forgive me for my occasional slip-ups, I wouldn't be here today.

We all fuck up. End of story.

We're the first ones here, and Charlie goes to the craft corner to start setting up the day's project for her, June, and Hayley to work on. It's all she talked about on the ride here, and I love her enthusiasm.

That leaves me and Tess alone, and the awkwardness between us now is grating. We need to move past this.

"So, are we still on for date number two on Friday?" I ask, trying desperately to stay cool, and not seem too eager. This has been a rollercoaster twenty-four hours, and the rise and fall of emotions is wearing me down. Between the high of yesterday morning, the low of Tess's post, the anger afterward, the grief of Dakota's story, the tenuous mending of me and Tess, to now – it's been a ride. And I think it's leaving me vulnerable.

Tess seems to be in the same boat, though, so at least we might be on an even emotional playing field. I'm sure she's had her own journey to deal with. In that at least, I'm not alone.

"I would like that," she says, biting her lip. "If you still want to."

I can't take it anymore and pull her into a hug. She tenses briefly, her muscles instinctively going rigid, but then melts against me, wrapping her arms around my back, her head leaning against my chest. Her heart is racing, and suddenly I want nothing more than to calm her down. Reassure her.

"We're good, babe. Okay?" I whisper. "We're good."

Her arms tighten around me as she nods, but she doesn't say anything. She's keeping her emotions in check better than I am right now. I can tell she wants to let loose another apology, but it isn't necessary. Not anymore. There's no malice here. Not with her.

Out of the corner of my eye I see Charlie looking over at us with a sly smile, and when I catch her and give her a wink, she automatically goes back to pretending she's busy setting up their project. She's not fooling me, though. I know she likes Tess, and the idea of us together.

Me too, kid. Me too.

twenty-four
falling

Tess

The guys are in the middle of working on a new song that Dakota and Brad have written, and Ian has taken his daughters to register for school in the fall, so it's me and Charlie left on the couch, playing Tic-Tac-Toe on the iPad while snacking on pretzels. She's kicking my ass, but I'm distracted by the song. It's heartbreaking and makes me wonder about the story behind it.

I still need to have a sit-down with Dakota to get his history, so I know what I'm dealing with press-wise. Eliza said they did a background check and things like that, which were fine, but there's always something getting ready to pop out of the woodwork. I need to know what it is before it shows itself. If this song is any indication, I'm in for some heavy emotions.

"I win again!" Charlie cheers, popping another pretzel in her mouth proudly.

"I think you're cheating," I say, clearing the screen for another round.

"Well, I think you're just bad at the game," she declares. Point taken.

"I think you're right," I smirk. "Want to play something else?"

"Nope."

I sigh. "Of course you don't. You're kind of murderizing me here. Not sure how I feel about your liking that..."

"My dad likes you," she whispers out of the blue, glancing over at the band.

I look over to make sure they're not paying attention to us, or at least didn't hear her.

"Well, I like your dad, too," I whisper back conspiratorially. It's starting to feel like a horribly kept secret. We're not necessarily hiding it from anyone, but there's still an air of secrecy around us. We sneak glances, and small touches, when we can if we think no one is looking. Chances are that we're wrong, and everybody knows.

"Are you going to go on another date?" Charlie asks, placing an 'X' on the game that blocks my win. Again.

"We are," I say distractedly, frowning at the game as I try to figure out a strategy to finally beat her. I'm starting to hate this game. "This Friday, actually. When you go for your next sleepover at Hayley and June's house."

"Aww. I wanted to go with you guys," she says, a small whine in her sweet voice.

I look over at her, an eyebrow arched. "You want to go on our date with us?" It seems like an odd request, but then, coming from Charlie, it's not really that out of character.

"Yeah. Remember that time we all went to dinner? And you guys were talking about work and stuff? I want to do that again." She takes another bite of a pretzel and wins yet another game with a tap of the screen.

Jesus, I suck at this game.

But Charlies request at least pulls my mind from the song the guys are working on. Would Brad want us to go out like that again? The three of us? After what happened yesterday with the post, I'm not sure. The hug he gave me earlier and his reassuring words make me think he might be open to it.

"Well, we'll have to ask your dad and see what he says," I finally admit. I don't want to promise her something that Brad would be against. I need to be very careful with how I handle Charlie. The last thing I want to do is cross another boundary that I can't see.

While things might be fine between us, I still feel like I'm walking a tight rope. Trying to balance work, the band, Brad, and his family, while not completely losing myself or screwing any of it up is starting to feel like more than I bargained for when I took this job. But then, I didn't expect to find myself falling for the singer, either. Or growing to really like his daughter.

I wonder if the walking on eggshells feeling will ever go away now that it's settled in.

The band wraps up for the day, and I corner Dakota briefly to set a time for us to chat tomorrow before rehearsal. I should have done this days ago, but it's better late than never. He's a little hesitant and is obviously uncomfortable about having to talk about his private life with me. Yesterday's incident must be affecting everyone after all. I don't know why I hadn't considered that prospect. Of course everyone would be affected by it.

After a little more convincing, he agrees to talk. I sigh inwardly with relief that I can at least make *some* progress. Getting his story and setting parameters around it about what can be public, and what can't, will get his introduction to fans off on the right foot. To be honest, I should have done that with everyone. Maybe I still should do that.

As I'm gathering my things to leave for the day, Charlie pulls Brad over to me by the hand, and his smile at her antics warms my heart.

"Daddy, Tess said we should all go to dinner tonight," she announces, and my mouth drops open.

"I did not say—" I start, shocked at her twisting of my words.

"Oh, really?" Brad asks, arching an eyebrow at me, knowing full well I didn't say that. I love that he's playing along with it, even though I was not prepared for this ambush.

Charlie bounces on her toes, excited that her scheming might be working. "Yup. She said we should all have dinner like last time. Maybe we could go to the same place and get burgers again!"

Her excitement is contagious, and I can't help the hope that wells up inside of me at the prospect of repeating our first dinner. It was when I initially took a real liking to Brad, seeing him interact with his daughter.

It made him a real person to me for the first time. I'd love to recapture that feeling again.

"I mean... I'm happy to go along with you guys if you want..." I stumble, still not sure that everything is mended between us. Yes, he said it was, but my guilt won't let me accept that completely yet.

"What are you talking about? Of course we do," Brad says, reaching out with his free hand, and taking mine. The three of us are now a linked chain, and it just feels *right*. There's no other word to describe it.

He leads us both toward the door, and Charlie leans back to peek at me behind her dad, her triumphant smile beaming. I can't help but beam right back at her.

She knows exactly what she's doing. And, God damn it, I don't mind it one bit. I should feel like a pawn being played on Charlie's chess board, but even if I am, I'm not going to complain.

I'm happy to be here.

twenty-five
the summoning

Brad

I know what's up. Charlie isn't fooling anybody, but I'm more than game to take Tess to dinner with us. It'll be like a pre-date date. A chance for us to break the icy wall that still feels like it lingers between Tess and me. I hate that it's there, but it is what it is. I also can't deny that I'm the one that built the damn thing in the first place.

As we're shown to our booth at the restaurant, Charlie positions herself on the end of a bench so that I need to sit next to Tess. Again, not complaining. I've wanted to get closer to her all day since our hug earlier anyway. Something about having her right next to me is calming somehow that makes no sense to my wrinkly brain, but I'm not about to fight it. Or Charlie.

After we order our drinks, we're all looking over the menus trying to decide on our meals, but I can feel Charlie staring at us. I debate internally whether to call her out on it. Staring isn't polite, or at least, that's what

I've been told, and the way she's doing it – trying not to get caught at it – keeps me from saying anything.

That is, until she starts being obvious about it.

"And what exactly are you staring at?" I ask, laying my menu on the table to give her my full attention. She blushes but doesn't look away. That's my Charlie.

"What? You two look cute together," she shrugs. Nothing but the truth from this girl.

Tess starts coughing next to me, nearly choking at Charlie's bluntness. It gives me the opportunity to reach over and pat her back gently, but then smoothly slide my arm around her shoulder and pull her against me. I like the way she feels in my arms.

"Do we now?" I look down at Tess next to me, who I can tell is embarrassed by this entire conversation. "What do you think, Tess? Do we make a cute couple?"

She starts coughing again, and luckily the server comes back with our drinks, from which Tess greedily grabs her glass of water and starts chugging it, stifling the onslaught. Deftly avoiding answering the question.

But Charlie's not done with us. Not by a long shot.

"Don't you think they make a cute couple?" She asks the server, a young woman in her early twenties with a long ponytail and a nose ring. Her nametag reads, 'Lauren.' And, until this question, she's been entirely disinterested in us.

She looks us both over, probably noticing that Tess is dying to crawl under the table and hide right now.

"You don't have to feed the monster," I say, giving Lauren an out from Charlie's antics. Nobody likes being put on the spot like this. Especially strangers. I need to run interference at times with Charlie when she gets this way, but the server apparently doesn't mind playing along.

"No, you guys are cute together," she says with a confident nod in our direction.

Tess hides her face in her hands, muttering, "Oh my God..." but my heart fucking swells at the approval of a total stranger. It makes no sense whatsoever, but it's like a confirmation of some kind that I didn't know I needed until right this very second.

"Well, thank you for that," I say, giving Tess's shoulder another squeeze and leaning in. "You hear that? We're cute."

"Can I just slide under the table really quick?" Tess asks, still covering her blushing face.

It's an innocent question. A completely, one-hundred percent, no doubt about it innocuous question, but man, my mind dives straight into the fucking gutter. A place it has no being in the middle of this family restaurant with my daughter across the God damned table. But just the thought...the idea...of Tess there... between my legs...

Fuck.

I clear my throat, grab my own water, and take a sip to try to stave off the dirty thoughts that are only growing more pervasive as they bounce around my brain.

"Anyway...we should probably order, huh?" I ask, reluctantly pulling my arm away from Tess to try to focus my brain on the task at hand.

Dinner. A family-friendly dinner. That's what we're here for.

Jesus Christ.

After dinner, which continues without further embarrassment by my conniving daughter, we drive Tess back to the studio to get her car. Charlie has gotten quiet during the ride, and as I park, I notice she's fallen asleep in the back seat. Tess and I glance at each other briefly, and my stomach tightens a little at having to end our time together already. It's too soon. And our official date on Friday can't come soon enough.

"I'll see you to your car," I say, opening my door, my voice low so as not wake Charlie.

As we walk to her car nearby, our hands are drawn together, our fingers intertwining. It's so fucking natural. So comfortable. So *us*. Something about the feeling makes me pull her to me, my hands framing her face as I lean in to kiss her.

I was only going for a chaste kiss goodnight, but when our lips brush against each other, an inferno ignites inside of me. As much as the lesser part of me wants to, I can't deny that I want Tess, in every way possible. And dinner tonight with the three of us only solidified that sentiment.

My fingers slide through her hair, and we lean against her car as our tongues dance, our breaths hitching, and our hearts racing in the same rhythm. The hunger inside of me that I'm perpetually fighting against is screaming to be satisfied, and I don't know how much longer I can tame it.

Being so close to Tess, every day, for hours at a time, is starting to drive me fucking crazy. And when she kisses me back like this, her body instinctively arching into mine, and her arms around my neck pulling me in - that restraint becomes even more difficult.

No, it's nearly impossible.

Tess must realize that we're getting carried away, too, because she pulls away. I can tell it's a bit reluctantly, and my chest tightens at the thought that she's as into this as I am. She glances over my shoulder to my car, where Charlie is still sleeping; blissfully unaware that her little matchmaking is paying off dividends.

"You should probably get sleepyhead over there to bed," she says with a smile, and God damn if I don't want to just start kissing her all over again.

I don't do it. But fucking hell, I want to.

So, I do have some self-control. *Nice.*

"Yeah," I say, half-heartedly, taking a step back to allow myself to take a breath. "Thanks for coming to dinner with us."

"Of course," she says, fishing for her keys in her purse. I can tell she's hiding her own disappointment at our having to end the evening. "I had a great time."

"Good," I say with an awkward nod. Since when am I awkward? I'm not awkward. What the fuck? "Text me when you get home."

And what, am I her father now, too? Wanting check-ins for safety? What the actual fuck is going on with me tonight? Or am I just slipping in and out of Dad-Mode? Is that even a thing?

Why am I questioning everything now?

Fucking hell.

I turn and head back to my car, feeling the frown on my face deepen as I ask myself these existential questions. There are too many flying around for me to focus on a single one of them.

When I get in, I glance up to the rearview mirror and catch Charlie looking back at me curiously but then quickly shut her eyes as if she were still sleeping.

Caught red handed.

"Nice try, baby girl," I say with a smirk. She's really outdoing herself lately.

"What?" she asks with a yawn, stretching as though she's just woken from a deep sleep.

"You're not fooling anyone, you know." I let Tess leave the lot first, then head toward my apartment, traffic light this time of evening for a change.

It takes a few minutes, but eventually her little voice pipes up behind me, soft but confident. "But is it working?"

The laugh that escapes me is uncontrollable. My little girl – my *baby girl* – is turning into some kind of diabolical matchmaker with plots and schemes for days to get me and Tess together. And fuck if it isn't working.

"Touché," I admit, shaking my head. "Touché."

twenty-six
like lovers do

Tess

Dakota is full of surprises. He's had a lot of life happen to him for such a young guy. I hate having to pry open old wounds for him, especially about his history of drug abuse, and the death of his wife, but if there's one thing I've learned in this business, it's that everything can and will be found out eventually. Things you thought you could keep to yourself, or that you think no one knows about, *will* become public fodder. Keeping anything from me will only make our lives harder once that happens.

Just knowing what skeletons are hiding in the closet allows me to prepare for whatever hell the public wants to make of them when they do become known. I know things about some well-respected people that would make your hair curl, but it's all a part of this job. Getting ahead of the story, before it becomes a scandal. If I'm not caught off guard, emergencies can be dealt with. And even with all of Dakota's skeletons, there's nothing unmanageable about them.

As a matter of fact, anyone who would try to spin his stories into anything other than the tragedies they are would be vilified for the attempt. He's had a hard life. And sure, some of the wounds have been self-inflicted, but that only adds to the tragicness of it all. My heart aches for him and all he's been through, but at the same time he's earned so much of my respect for how he's getting through it. He's chosen to rise above his circumstances and try for better things, to be a better person, make the world a better place. I admire that spirit and wish I had more of that in my own attitude.

When comparing his to what I think is my own hard life, it's put into perspective. Everyone goes through their own shit, and we all think it's the worst. Then you hear stories like Dakota's, and you realize how much worse it really could have been. Not that you feel lucky, that's not the point. But you do start to feel how alike we all are in our suffering. Because no matter what that shit is you've gone through, the emotional reaction and fallout is the same, or at least similar.

We all hurt. We all have been hurt. We all have hurt others, whether it was intentional or not. Pain is universal. Some are deeper and longer lasting, but no less the same. Some people can brush it off, while others dwell on it and marinate in their pain for long periods of time, or even for the rest of their lives. And some just can't deal with it at all.

Dakota went through all of it but seems to have

landed in a healthy head space. I give him a lot of credit for ending up here, when his own life could have ended as just another tragic story. His emotional strength feels limitless.

When we're done talking, I feel emotionally wrung out, like my heart is both overflowing and empty at the same time.

"Thanks for sharing your story with me," I say, meeting Dakota's eyes with sincerity. "I know it wasn't easy to bare your soul like this so early in the morning."

And by early in the morning, I mean it's just before noon. For a rockstar, this is the crack of fucking dawn. And being interrogated about your life isn't the easiest thing to do no matter what time of day it is.

"I get it," he nods, tucking a strand of long dark hair behind his ear. "I get why you need to know this stuff. No worries."

"Well, just know that until something comes out directly from you, or we need to react to something external, what you've told me stays between us, okay? Consider me a vault of secrets."

"Duly noted," he chuckles, and the sense of relief in that laugh tells me all I need to know about him. He's told me everything and kept nothing back.

There's always a worry that there's something, some small minute detail that's just waiting in the shadows to reveal itself when you least expect it, and always at the most inopportune time. Not with Dakota. That small release of worry in his tone tells me that he has bared his soul. There's nothing left to share with me. And knowing that makes me relax a little bit. I'm prepared to deal with whatever the world might throw at him, and I'll be his most ardent defender.

Let them try.

On Friday, the entire practice space seems to be bubbling with extra energy. There are sparks in the air as if everyone knows Brad and I are having our second official date. Obviously, they don't, since we still haven't said anything about it to anyone, but it feels like everyone knows something is going on.

And I don't care. At least not about the inner circle. Not about the Chaos Fuel family. What I do care about is the public, and what it would mean if their fans found out. Of all people, I know how it would look to an outsider to see Brad hooking up with someone he works with. It will not go well.

So, for that reason, our date tonight is at my place. And I'm cooking us dinner.

I am not the best cook, *but* I'm also not the worst. I have a few signature dishes that I've mastered over the years. I've conquered a million ways to spice up ramen, and can scramble eggs like a pro. That just goes with living alone and having to cook for yourself most of the time.

Cooking for two? For a date? That's a different story. My go-to dish is lasagna. It's basically foolproof if you get the right ingredients, and the leftovers are often better than the original meal. The problem is that I don't know how to make a small lasagna for two, so I end up making an entire deep dish pan of it and will most likely be eating lasagna for the rest of the foreseeable future.

I'm also not the neatest cook. Some people clean as they go – I am not them. By the time the lasagna goes into the oven, my kitchen looks like a disaster area of dishes, utensils, cheese containers, and tomato sauce. Glancing around, and then down at myself, I find that I'm also covered in tomato sauce.

Fuck.

I tried to be so neat, and even had one of my grandmother's old aprons on, but the sauce found a way to aim around it and hit my carefully selected outfit. There's even some in my hair. How did that even get there?

Swearing to myself under my breath, I hurry to clean everything up. The kitchen, the dishes, myself. The entire time I'm praying and wishing for Brad to take his time. In my head, I've still got at least fifteen minutes.

Don't be early. Please don't be early.

The doorbell rings.

Shit. Fuck balls. Criminy on a cracker.

Of course, he's early.

I rip the apron off, and ball it up, throwing it into a drawer I'll forget about later. Running down the hall to my bedroom, I nearly bang into the wall as I pull my shirt over my head blindly. I hurry to find another blouse, and button it up quickly, making sure it matches my skirt. Taking a quick glance in the mirror by the door, I do my best to pull myself together, my heart racing a mile a minute.

I don't even look through the peephole, and swing the door open, my breath labored from running around, but all I see are flowers. Bouquet upon bouquet of flowers. Is this a delivery or something?

"What the—?"

Brad peeks through between the bouquets, a sheepish grin on his face.

"I wasn't sure what kind of flowers you liked...so I got some of each..."

My hand is on my chest as if it can keep the racing to a minimum, but it's not working. I can't believe he bought out a damned florist shop for me.

For me.

After the past week, I thought we might still be awkward alone, but this – this douses all those thoughts. He really has forgiven my mistake, and fucking hell, he's hitting this date out of the park at the first bat.

"Brad...you shouldn't have..." I say as I start taking the flowers from him.

"Actually, I can't take all the credit," he says, following me into my now spotless kitchen that smells amazing. "It was mostly Charlie's idea."

"To buy every flower in LA?" I search for vases in my cupboards. I think I have one or two... I know I don't have enough for all of these.

"Well, to bring you flowers. Once I got to the florist, and they asked what kind, I kind of went a little crazy." His cheeks flush red at the admission, and holy shit, I don't know if I can make it through dinner without throwing myself at him.

"A little? There's a contender for Understatement of the Year." I can't help but laugh as I start trying to cram every flower into some sort of arrangement in the three vases I was able to find. "I don't have enough vases for all of these..."

"Let me see," he says, rummaging through the cabinets and pulling out tall glasses and travel water bottles while grinning. "Improvisation at its finest."

We work side by side in a comfortable silence, cutting stems, pulling off extra leaves, sorting the flowers into various containers. The fragrance of the flowers mixed with the aroma of spicy Italian food is heady, but delightful. There's a charge bouncing between us as we work. An undercurrent that accentuates our closeness in the small footprint of my kitchen.

"Ouch," I hiss, as my thumb catches on a rose's thorn, a small bead of blood rising on the skin.

I instinctively bring it to my mouth to suck on, but Brad reaches over and grabs my wrist, pulling me close. He catches and holds my gaze as he licks the blood from my finger. Heat shoots through me as I watch, the sting of the cut instantly gone, and other sensations jumping to the surface.

"Better?" he asks, still locking eyes with me as he turns my hand, exposing my palm, and proceeds to trace a trail of kisses across my wrist, my pounding pulse nearly evident on the thin skin where his lips brush. His soft beard almost tickles as it touches.

"Much," I breathe, forgetting all about the thorn, and concentrating instead on his lips on my body. I want them all over me.

Now.

I break free of his hold and grab his shirt in a fist to pull him to me. His eyebrows raise briefly in surprise, but then his lips start to curve into a smile. I don't let that smile finish as I take his mouth with mine, pouring my need into him with a kiss that could set this apartment on fire.

My hands are in his hair, and his are in mine, our lips locked and our bodies arching into each other with desire. It's clear that we both want the same thing, and we're both clear on the timing.

Now.

twenty-seven
middle of the night

Brad

I didn't mean to start this fire, but fuck if I'm going to stop it now. When Tess pulls me to her, instinct and passion take over, and I want to feel every inch of her. My palms itch to slide against her bare skin, to grab her curves and fit mine to hers.

She reaches for my shirt, pulling it effortlessly over my head, and then her mouth is on my chest while her nails rake lightly over my skin. I can't help the shudder that runs through me as I press against her, and into the counter. The hardness of my cock grows as my hands find her breasts, the nipples erect and straining against her bra.

It needs to go. And her blouse too. Off they come.

Well, not without *some* difficulty. My fucking hands are shaking, and I don't know why. Am I fucking nervous? It's not like I don't know how to fuck. I've done this more than a few times, but something feels different with Tess. This feels important somehow in a way I can't explain.

"Need some help there?" she giggles as she notices me struggling with a particularly stubborn button.

"Fucking hush, woman," I laugh. "I know what I'm doing, alright?"

The stupid fucking button won't budge. It's got to be witchcraft. Or a trick of some kind. A mindfuck of ultimate proportions. The final boss in a video game. The definitive cock block.

Sure, take my shirt off...if you can...

"You sure you don't want some help?" she asks, her hands wandering to the front of my jeans. The sharp inhale that escapes me when she drags her fingers along the outline of my erection is loud in the small space.

I let go of the resistant button and grab her hips, pulling to grind myself against her. The sensation running through me is electrifying, but it's not enough.

"What I want, is to be inside you," I whisper into her ear, unable to control my words, or my desire. This woman is making me fucking insane with simple touches. I've not felt that before. I can't get enough of her, and I want her to feel the same. "You're driving me to madness here..."

It's her turn to gasp as my fingers deftly pull up her miniskirt and drag between her legs. While I'm surprised to find her bare underneath, it's a pleasant surprise, and one that makes me even harder.

"Oh, but we're all mad here," she says, pulling on her

blouse and ripping it open for me, the evil button pinging off into the hell it belongs in.

Given access to her chest, I take full advantage, caressing one breast while feasting on the other. Her skin is so soft, it almost feels like it's never been touched. Well, it's never been touched by *me*, and I plan to explore all of it.

Her hand slides into my jeans, and wraps around my cock, the touch almost too much for me to take. It's too perfect. It's too soon. It's not enough.

My thoughts jumble as I grab her hips again and lift her onto the counter, sending flower debris flying, but I don't care. I need this woman; stupid buttons and flowers be damned.

"Are we doing this?" I ask, trying to catch my breath as I come up for air. We're both panting and shaking, whether nerves or anxiousness, I don't know, but we're in this together at least.

She studies me for only a heartbeat, then nods. "We better be. Do you have a condom?"

I don't need a heartbeat to whip out my wallet and pull one out. This gets us both breaking out in laughter again, and the sound echoes off the kitchen walls. It's music.

It doesn't get better than this.

She sheathes me, and I almost come right then. Somehow, I hold it back. But when I slide into her, wet and inviting, I know this first time of ours isn't going to last long. I've dreamt about this too many times for it not to affect me, so I make sure to see to it that she enjoys this too.

I bite lightly on her nipple, while my thumb traces circles on her clit, keeping my movements slow and deliberate as best as I can. What I want is to speed up. Chase the orgasm. But somewhere I find patience. Not a lot of it, but enough.

I can feel her tighten around my cock, and her legs wrap around me, pulling me in deeper with each thrust of my hips. I can't hold it back anymore.

"Come for me, babe," I order, kissing her deeply as I move inside her. Giving her the friction she needs to meet me. "Come for me now."

Her body tenses, and every muscle tightens as she explodes around me. She wants to cry out, but I've still got her trapped in my kiss, taking it for myself as I erupt along with her. Both of us shudder for a long moment as the pleasure courses through us, then we relax. No, more than that - we collapse into each other's arms, our breaths uneven.

Our heightened state deflates into an afterglow that seems to radiate from the two of us. That was perfection. Even in all my imaginings of us together, it was never that good. This is going to be hard to beat. But, fuck, if I'm not willing to try.

"Holy shit," Tess says in a half-whisper, half-sigh, half-laugh. Fuck math, it's beautiful. She's beautiful. Her skin is flushed and there's a slight sheen of sweat on her forehead and chest. She's the most amazing being I've ever seen.

Whoa. Easy there, cowboy.

"Was that alright?" I ask, floundering for words to put in the right order that make any sort of sense. I know it was, because I could feel that it was, but obviously, my brain is currently compromised.

She smacks me playfully on the chest. "You're kidding, right? That was amazing."

Still inside her, I kiss her and grab her ass and give one long final thrust. Just a taste of what more there is ahead of us. Because fucking hell, there had better be more of this.

A lot more.

twenty-eight
beside myself

Tess

So, Brad's got some surprises up his sleeve too. Noted.

Very much appreciated, and noted, that is. Holy shit that was amazing. I was hoping for something along these lines for dessert, but never did I anticipate it being the appetizer. Of course, now, my actual appetite has kicked in, and as we're cleaning up my stomach grumbles loudly.

Brad comes up behind me, sliding his arms around my waist as he nuzzles into my neck. It's simply delicious, and something I could get used to. "Now that right there's a hunger I unfortunately can't satisfy." His short whiskers tickle my skin as he trails kisses along my shoulder.

"Don't worry your pretty head, I've got dinner covered," I say, leaning back into him. I'd melt right here and now into a puddle on the floor if I could. But then, neither of us would eat, so there's that.

"Pretty head, huh?" he chuckles, his breath warm on my exposed skin, as his long hair drapes over me. "You think I'm pretty?"

"I think you're beautiful, yeah," I say before thinking about what words are coming out of my mouth. Once what I said hits me, I freeze. I'm not lying, but it might be a bit much. Too much too soon.

"No, *you're* beautiful," he says, spinning me back around and pulling his t-shirt over my head, then straightening it. Something in his eyes when he says and does this makes the butterflies in my chest go berserk. Compliments are one thing, but when they're said with that much emotion and conviction, it makes me want to believe he means it.

"Thank you," I say quietly, lifting on my toes to kiss him. It's all I can think of to say, and I can barely get the words out I'm so taken with him. As he pulls me into a deeper kiss, my mind starts to whirl.

What is going on here? I've slept with hot guys before. I've been in relationships with passionate people. Most of them turned out to be assholes, sure, but at the time I thought it was special. This is different somehow, and I don't know what it is. This feels deeper in a way that I can't describe. Like we'd never be able to reach the bottom of the well of emotions between us. It's daunting and exhilarating at the same time.

I want to see where this goes because I think it could be something amazing. Something mind blowing. And not just the sex, as incredible as it was. Something real is sparking between us now, and once it ignites, I get the feeling we'd be unstoppable.

When we finally break apart and come up for air once again, it takes me a minute to pull myself together. I could easily lose myself in all things Brad – his charisma and charm, his sex appeal, his humor, his...everything. Do I really want to do that? Lose myself? Would it really be that bad if I did? Isn't that what's held me back before? Fear of letting myself go and just letting someone love me?

It is. I've been known to self-sabotage like the best of them. Well, when I wasn't getting fucked over, at least. It's either one or the other, and it makes me wonder which one this is going to be since that's all there apparently is.

No, I refuse to self-sabotage this. I'm going to let this be whatever it is, because I can tell it will be worth it in the end.

If that's true, then why is there a little voice in the back of my head telling me to be careful? Guard my heart? Keep the walls up just a little bit longer to see how things play out without getting too wrapped up in it?

Shut up little voice. I'm not listening to you.

twenty-nine
pillowtalk

Brad

I'm buying Charlie a fucking pony.

I don't know for sure if it was her idea of the flowers that tipped things over the edge, or what, but God damn, that was the best fucking date I've ever had in my life.

Great sex, great food and conversation, then even more great sex in the shower. All in that order. Even the few hours of sleep that we nabbed were enough to make me feel truly rested. I haven't felt that in a long time. What a perfect night.

And now, it's turned into a perfect morning. After dozing on and off in between a mind-numbing blow job, and then returning the favor, I can hear Tess in the kitchen trying to be quiet while making coffee. She's failing at that miserably as I hear silverware clatter to the tile floor followed by a mutter curse.

Fucking hell, she's a dream come true.

I debate laying here, and letting Tess come to me

with coffee, but like a lodestone, I'm automatically drawn to her wherever she is. So, I drag my ass out of bed, throw on my jeans, and hang in the doorway to the kitchen, silently watching her sing quietly to herself as she makes coffee, her hips swaying sensually to the beat of the music only she can hear. She has her earbuds in and hasn't noticed me yet.

I love that I'm seeing her with her guard down, when she thinks no one is watching. Her blonde hair is a bedhead mess, but sexy as fuck. *I* messed up that hair, and it's like a fucking badge of honor to see her this way. Her lips are a little swollen from all our kisses, and again – *I* did that. Signs of me are all over her, and I fucking love it.

"Good morning," I say in a normal tone because I don't know how loud her music is in her ears since I can't hear it. I don't want to startle her.

Nothing.

The singing and dancing continue, so I just let her go on in her obliviously happy place. I lean further back and cross my arms, enjoying the show. Waking up to this every day wouldn't be a bad way to live a life.

She must catch the movement out of the corner of her eye because she jumps about two feet off the ground with a yelp. I hurry over to stop her from backing into the refrigerator, my laughter erupting as I pull her into a bear hug.

"You scared the shit out of me," she yells over the music still in her ears.

I pull out one of the earbuds and stick it in my own

ear. It's Murderous Crows' latest song playing, and I'm not sure if I should be offended it's not Chaos Fuel she's listening to. I decide to let it slide just this once...

"Sorry, babe. You were too fucking cute to interrupt." I nuzzle into her neck, inhaling her sweet scent as if it sustains me. Maybe it does. I can't imagine being without it now.

"I was trying to be quiet and not wake you," she says, a giggle playing in her voice as I squeeze her tighter.

"And I was enjoying the show," I say, nibbling on her ear as I walk her backward toward the bedroom. "You look good in my shirt."

"Oh yeah?"

"Yeah. But you look better out of it..."

thirty
the bliss

Tess

B rad just left to pick up Charlie, and I'm meeting Ivy for lunch. My mind is still reeling from the amazing night Brad and I just had, and I can't quite put it into perspective. I've never felt like this about someone before.

Bliss. I've never felt bliss before.

I've been happy, sure. Even ecstatic. But never bliss. Things have never felt 'perfect' in any relationship I've had. And to be honest, it's kind of scaring the shit out of me.

"Girl, you are giving off weird honeymoon vibes. What's up with that?" Ivy asks after giving me a hug in the restaurant, her eyes flashing with mischief.

I sit across from her and grin, but even I can feel the fear emanating from me. "Honeymoon vibes?" I consider that. It did feel a bit like a honeymoon. It was only one night, but it was intense. I nod my head from side to side, trying not to let my doubts invade my thoughts and ruin everything. "That's not too far off the mark."

"So, what's off, then? I get the feeling you're not telling me something." Ivy's long dark hair, and intelligent dark eyes always gives her a mystical sort of aura, and when she reads me so clearly like this, it's only accentuated.

Debating this within myself is going to get me nowhere, fast. So, I give in. "It's almost *too* perfect, you know?"

"Is that a real thing?"

"Of course, it is. I've never felt this good with someone. There's got to be something wrong with it. Something's going to come along and pop this bubble. And whatever it is, is going to devastate me." Saying it out loud makes me feel better, at least. It's a scary thing to share your fears with someone, but I know I can trust Ivy.

She leans across the table and pats my hand comfortingly. "Babe, the bubble always bursts. But that's life. That's reality. Even honeymoons don't last forever. The world just doesn't work that way. Enjoy this one while it lasts."

"Okay, it may not last forever, but how do I make it last longer? I don't want to face reality yet." I laugh, but it's forced. And it's the truth – I don't want this feeling to end, even though it's mixed with fear that it will.

"Just keep doing whatever it is you're doing. It's obviously working." A sly smile creeps into her mischievous expression. "I have a feeling there's a lot of killer sex involved..."

The flush on my cheeks is immediate, and I glance around as if everyone else in the restaurant heard what Ivy said. They didn't, of course, but just flashing back to memories of last night and this morning is enough to make me a little heated.

"There may have been..." While I'm not shy, I'm also not one to kiss and tell. I keep that part of my private life very private. "And that's all you get."

Ivy pouts as she leans back and crosses her arms. "You're no fun."

I arch a brow, still remembering a particularly hot moment from this morning, when Brad led me back to the bedroom after finding me dancing in the kitchen. The things he did to me...

"That's not what Brad said this morning..." My grin gives me away.

"You naughty, naughty, girl," Ivy sings, taking a sip of her mimosa. "God, I wish you weren't so tight-lipped about that stuff. I need to live vicariously through you."

As we chat about our love lives over lunch, I try my best to keep the bubble of relationship perfection around me going and ignore the nagging voice in my head telling me to be wary. But it doesn't work.

My internal insecurities aren't allowing me to enjoy this fully, and it's bugging the shit out of me. Why can't I let myself be happy for once? Just enjoy the high of falling in love.

Wait. Is that what I'm doing? Am I falling in love with Brad Chambers?

Shit. Shit. Shit. I think I am.

I wave down our server.

"Can I get another mimosa?"

thirty-one
a crooked melody

Brad

When I go to pick up Charlie from Ian's house, I find Mackenzie Roberts there, his girlfriend, and band manager for Murderous Crows. They're in the middle of planning their day, and apparently an amusement park is on the menu.

Standing in lines in the hot sun for lame rides was not on my bingo card for the day. While I did get some restful sleep, it wasn't enough to sustain me through whatever playful hell they're conjuring up.

Mackenzie must take in my lack of enthusiasm for the outing. "We'd be happy to take Charlie with us and keep her overnight again. Wouldn't we girls?" She turns to June and Hayley, who immediately start jumping and cheering at the idea.

I appreciate that Mac didn't include the *'if you don't want to go'* part of her statement. It's not that I don't want to spend time with my daughter – of course, it's not that. There's just a certain mindset you need to be in for that kind of day, and I'm not there.

Turning to Charlie to get her input, I see the excitement written all over her face at the prospect of the outing. My chest tightens at the thought of ever disappointing her. I can't do it. I'd give her the moon and the stars if she asked for it. I'd find a way. It's clear in her hopeful expression that she wants to go on this adventure with her friends. I can't say no.

"Are you sure you want to spend the day with your friends, having fun, eating junk food, riding rollercoasters, and other amazing stuff?" I keep my face as straight as possible, but she's onto me. "Instead of hanging with your boring old man, watching bird documentaries, inside a stuffy apartment?"

"Hmm...I don't know..." she plays along, rubbing her chin thoughtfully.

"I know it's tempting and all but use your best judgement."

Poor June and Hayley can't tell if we're playing a game or not. They actually look worried that Charlie will choose me over them. Silly girls. Ian and Mackenzie really need to work on teaching them sarcasm.

Charlie sighs dramatically, adding sympathy to her tone. She's too good at this. "Sorry, Dad. I'm going to have to go with these guys today. I'll see you tomorrow though."

I let out my own defeated sigh, playing up my pitiful expression. I run a hand through my hair and scratch my head. "Fine. I get it. I'm just a boring dad. You guys have fun, I guess."

There's an awkward beat before Charlie and I burst out laughing, and she runs into me, hugging my waist.

"You're the best, Dad," she giggles.

"Yeah, yeah. Just don't give Ian and Mac any trouble, got it?" I say, kneeling to hug her back.

"We'll take good care of her," Ian says, wrapping an arm around Mackenzie. The two of them are turning into quite a power couple at Blackmore, and I love to see it. "I'll give you a status update on our adventure later."

"Sounds good," I say, heading back to my car. On the way, I get a text from Stefan.

> STEFAN: We're hitting the Whisky
> tonight. Lizzy's band is playing.
> You in?

I haven't thought that far ahead yet since my plan to have Charlie tonight literally just changed. My mind instantly goes to Tess, and my first reaction is to maybe see what she's up to instead. I wouldn't mind a repeat of last night if possible.

> ME: Possibly. I'll keep you posted.

"Have you been day drinking?" I ask Tess on the phone a little later. I've been trying to reach her for a few hours now so that I can figure out what I'm doing tonight. She took a while to answer, and she's giggling like crazy. I can hear her friend Ivy in the background laughing as well.

At least one of us is having a good time.

"Maybe..." she laughs, and the cutest fucking snort I've ever heard bursts out of her, which only sends her and her friend into further laughter.

I wish like hell I was there to witness this cuteness in person. But I get it. We both need time with our friends. We don't want to burn too hot with each other only to fizzle out into nothingness later. That would royally suck.

"Okay, okay," I say, not wanting to interfere with their fun. "You ladies have fun, okay? I'm going to go hang with the guys tonight. I'll call you tomorrow?"

"Aww, I wanna hang with the guys, too..." she whines, as if she's going to miss something exciting, and again, it's adorable. Part of me wishes she would come too, just so I could see her like this in person. Tipsy Tess sounds hard to resist.

"What am I? Chopped burger? Hamburger? Ham? Liver?" Ivy calls from the background, and they both explode into laughter again.

As their laughter goes on, I almost think Tess forgets she's on a call with me, but she comes back eventually.

"Brad? Brad? Are you there?" Now she sounds worried, and that too does something to my heart. Even in her alcohol infused haze, she's worried about me.

"I'm here, but I'm going to let you go have fun with Ivy, okay?" I need to let her have her friend time.

"Okay," she slurs, a little sad. "I'll call you Thursday."

"Sounds good," I chuckle before hanging up. That was hilarious, and again my heart pangs that I'm not seeing it live and in person. It was about to turn melancholy, and seeing Tess all sappy would have seriously made my day.

I guess I'm on my own tonight.

When I get to the Whisky, the guys are already here. Even Dakota made it and is sipping a soda next to Emmett. He's fitting in nicely with all of us, in his quiet way. It complements our crazy in a way that another crazy couldn't. I like it.

"What, no Tess?" Stefan asks, eyebrow raised. I can't tell if he's kidding around, or fishing for information. Do they already know about me and Tess?

I thought we've done pretty well, keeping it from everyone that we're seeing each other, but I guess I was wrong. Maybe everyone knows already. Suddenly my emotions are mixed, and I don't know why. Do I not want people to know about us?

"Nope. No Tess," I say, not confirming or denying anything. I don't want to give them fuel to start shit about it.

"You two are a thing now, right?" Emmett asks, always the nosey fucker. "Well, for now. Your newest victim?"

"Victim?" I ask, not liking his tone one bit. I may have been a player in the past, but that's not who I am anymore. At least, that's what I keep telling myself. Things with Tess are different.

Right?

"You know what I mean, man," Emmett continues, though I wish he would shut the fuck up. "You're not exactly known for your solid relationship skills."

"Oh, and you are?" I wave down the bartender and order a shot and a beer. I can tell already this is going to be a long night.

"Pfft, fuck no. But at least I know myself." He looks at Stefan and Dakota for back up, but they don't seem to be interested in getting involved in this. Good for them. It doesn't deter him from continuing. "A leopard can't change its spots, dude. You are who you are. Just admit it and embrace it."

His words hit home, and I down my shot and chase it with the beer. It burns going down, but at least it's a feeling. A sensation. Something other than the small voice in my head that wants to agree with everything Emmett has said.

Maybe there's some truth to what he's saying. I'm not boyfriend material. Hell, the only material I'm made of are ragged strings, trying to sew themselves together to make some sort of recognizable shape. I don't know if it's working.

What I do know is that my feelings for Tess are different from anything else I've experienced before. With other women it was all surface and zero depth. With Tess I seem to have an insatiable appetite. And not just for sex, as amazing as that is, but for everything about her. I want to know everything.

But is it just infatuation? She's so different from everyone else I've dated that it's a novelty of some kind? And it's going to wear off at some point in the future when I least expect it? It's possible, sure, but that doesn't feel right either.

And why the fuck am I trying to put it into some sort of box? Categorize or label it to fit some sort of algorithm in my head? Hell, even my heart? And why the fuck am I questioning everything now?

Fuck Emmett.

"You don't know the first thing about it, dude," I say, pushing my shot glass to the edge of the bar for a refill. The bartender gives me the familiar nod of acknowledgement. "People *can* change." I turn on the barstool to face him head-on. "*You* just choose not to."

He laughs, "Me? Change? Why would I even want to? I'm great. Fucking fantastic as I am."

Stefan and I catch each other's eyes and start laughing at the ridiculousness of Emmett's statement. He's the worst out of all of us; never taking a damn thing seriously – especially relationships.

"Dude, you've never even had a girlfriend," I chide. He has no clue what he's talking about.

"Why would I want that hassle? That ball and chain?" he scoffs, as if it's the most preposterous idea in the world, and I'm insane for even suggesting it. "I am free as a bird to do whatever the fuck I want, with whoever the fuck I want, whenever the fuck I want. Don't mess with success, man. You remember those days, right? Wasn't it just a few months ago when you broke up with Gina that you were cruising Sunset right next to me? How quickly you forget..."

"It was more than a few months ago," I argue, not liking the picture he's painting of me as some kind of poster boy for failed relationships. He's not entirely wrong. That was me. But it's not anymore. "And I haven't forgotten shit. Trust me. But people can and do change – if they want to. And, you know what? I do."

Emmett must sense something in me, maybe it's the truth he's finally seeing, who knows, but his eyes shine as if he's trying to think of a comeback.

Before he can find one, Dakota chimes in, making all of us turn to look at him. "People can change, like Brad said. I know that I've changed a lot in the last few years. It's not easy, but it's doable, you know?"

Stefan and I nod our agreement, though I think I'm the only one of us that really knows about his wife dying, and the story behind it. Emmett, on the other hand, gives Dakota a resentful sideways glance for butting in.

"What the fuck would you know about it?" Emmett sneers. "You're what, barely twenty-one?"

"I'm twenty-six," he says, and I can see a little bit of anger peeking through.

Good. Let him have it, kid.

"No way," Emmett waves him off.

Dakota apparently doesn't like being dismissed like that, and stands up, his height now prominent compared to Emmett's, who starts to shrink a little bit at the display.

"Way. And trust me, I *do* know what it's like to be in a relationship, *and* to change." His brows draw down and I can see the pain behind the anger that's now surfacing. This is about to get out of hand.

Leave it to Emmett to do this tonight. It was supposed to be a fun night out, and it's turned into a shitshow already. I'm not drunk enough to deal with this bullshit.

"Guys let's just drop it, and enjoy the show," I say, lifting my hands in surrender. I hate that I always have to play mediator between Emmett and whoever he's decided to fuck with, but I've played this role long enough to know when it's needed. Like now. "When is Lizzy's band starting?"

Stefan glances at his phone. "About fifteen minutes, I'd guess."

Dakota takes the cue and sits back down at the bar, while Emmett takes a chug of his beer, nonplussed by everything he just stirred up.

I, on the other hand, can't get Emmett's words out of my head. Downing the newly provided shot, I try to push the negativity away but it's fucking persistent. I talked a good talk, but do I believe it? Why am I suddenly doubting everything again?

Glancing over at Dakota, I wonder about what he's said. Sure, maybe he has changed from who he was back when his wife died, but what good is it really doing him? It doesn't seem like he's really moved on from her death.

He's cleaned himself up, but it's not like he's putting himself out there to test it. What if he can't have another relationship like the one he had with his wife?

What if I can't handle a real relationship? My spots may have changed, but what if they're still in the same place? I could be stuck being a surface guy, just chasing the high of new things. And maybe that's all I'm doing with Tess, and it just feels different because she's a different kind of person than who I usually date. She just has her shit together.

I'll fuck it up somehow. Of that, I'm sure. If life has taught me anything, it's that I can't have nice things. I'll find a way to break any new toy that I get, just like the fucking man-child that I am.

What if Emmett is right?

thirty-two
prayers

Tess

I spend most of Sunday laying on the couch, trying not to move too suddenly, and praying that the medicine I took for my headache doesn't upset my stomach too much. Ivy is on the loveseat across from me, hugging a throw pillow, looking a little green in the gills herself.

"Why do we do this to ourselves?" she moans, staring at the TV that's on with the sound off and subtitles on.

"I don't know," I groan back. "It used to be fun."

"Why do our bodies hate us?"

"That's a great question. I'm starting to hate mine right back."

"Remember when we used to be able to go to the club, drink until we were puking in the ladies' room, holding each other's hair, fixing stranger's boy problems, clean ourselves up, and then go right back for more?" She takes a slow sip of her bottled water. "We used to be able to wake up the next day, and the worst thing would be we went to bed with makeup on, and we'd have raccoon eyes from all the fucking mascara. Not this entire body betrayal bullshit."

"That was like ten years ago. And to be fair, we did drink a lot yesterday," I murmur, trying not to move my head too much. My eyes are still closed because even the dim sunlight peeking around the drawn curtains is way too much for me to handle. "How much did we drink?"

"I didn't think it was enough for me to feel this bad."

"Me neither."

Our afternoon lunch turned into full blown day-drinking, which I am decidedly *not* used to. I'm a glass of wine, or maybe a few beers with dinner kind of girl. Not a full-day and into the night drinker. But, I guess, once in a while letting loose with your best friend is called for. And to be honest, it *was* fun.

Obviously, we're paying the price for it now, though. I guess I've hit the age where I'm not going to bounce back like I used to. I'm only thirty-one for God's sake. It doesn't feel like an age where this kind of deterioration should be happening yet. Isn't this supposed to be my prime? Or at least close to it?

I start replaying the highlights of yesterday's binge, including my call with Brad. He seemed so amused to hear me tipsy on the phone. Ivy didn't help the situation with her cracking me up while we talked. I wonder how his evening out with the band went.

Slowly reaching over blindly to the coffee table, I pat around for my phone. Secretly, I'm hoping to find messages from him, telling me how much he missed me last night, or was thinking of me. Instead, when I carefully ease my eyes open and start scrolling through my phone, I see a bunch of messages from me to him – unanswered.

My stomach lurches.

Oh no.

I did the drunk girl thing.

Fuck.

> 9:37PM ME: Hey there. Thinking about you. Hope you're having fun.

> 10:02PM ME: Ivy said to say hi. So, hi. ☺

> 10:33PM ME: I guess you're busy having fun! Thinking about you.

> 11:11PM ME: It's 11:11. I think that means something. Anyway, hope you're good.

> 11:12PM ME: Sorry, I'm a little drunk. I'll shut up now.

> 12:15AM ME: Are you mad at me? Or just not looking at your phone. It's okay. I understand.

> 12:50AM ME: <3

> 1:36AM ME: ☹ I miss you.

"Oh. My. God." I feel like I'm going to be sick. I did not turn into some pitiful, needy, bitch of a girlfriend last night, did I? I did. I totally fucking did.

"What?" Ivy asks, lifting her head slightly in my direction.

I toss my phone back onto the coffee table, the clattering sound hurting my brain. What the fuck is wrong with me lately?

"I did the thing," I say, wiping my hands down my face in despair.

"What thing?"

"The stupid drunk clingy girlfriend thing."

"Oh," she says, realizing what I'm getting at. "Oh no."

"Yup. I totally did it. I can't believe it, but it's all right there. Shit."

"And how did he respond?" She asks, curiosity laced with humor in her tone. I don't appreciate the humor. This isn't funny.

And then it hits me.

He didn't respond.

At all.

"He didn't." The finality of it rings hollow in the quiet room, and I can feel the weight of it pressing down on me.

Ivy is quiet. Ivy never gets quiet.

"Oh," is all she says.

I turn my head to look at her, and she meets my gaze. I instantly see the remorse in her eyes. She's thinking the same thing I am. It was way too early to celebrate anything last night, least of all my budding relationship with Brad.

We jumped the gun. And my constant texting really

didn't help at all either. If anything, it probably pushed him away even quicker.

Way to go Lagerfeld. You really know how to fuck things up, don't you?

"I'm a fixer. I can fix this, right?" I ask, trying to force confidence I don't feel.

Ivy's not buying it, and I don't blame her. This is bad.

"Sure," she says, and the sarcasm in her tone hits the mark. We both know this is yet another major screw up by me in all things Chaos Fuel, and specifically Brad.

Since day one, I've done nothing but mishandle and mismanage my feelings for Brad. I've let them cloud my professional judgement, and now, even my personal actions. This is not me. This is not who I am.

I'm becoming some hormone-injected pre-pubescent teenage girl with my first boy crush, losing all my sensibilities. All of a sudden, I'm impulsive, when I'm usually strategic and thoughtful. I examine every angle before acting on anything. Now, I just let whims carry me away and do whatever the hell I feel like in the moment.

Well, look where that got me. Absolutely nowhere.

Can I blame Brad though? After the video incident, and now the drunken text barrage, he's probably running for the hills. I thought we shared something special the other night, but maybe it was all one-sided. Maybe it was just me that felt something click between us. Maybe he met someone else last night at the show? Or ran into yet another old flame still carrying a torch for him that he was drawn to.

We haven't talked about exclusivity, because why would we? We've technically only been on two official dates. I have no claim on him. He's free to see whoever he wants, isn't he?

I'd swear he was feeling for me what I'm feeling for him, but like everything else in my life right now, I could be reading that all wrong. I could be reading more into it.

My head starts pounding even harder, the blood pulsing in my ears. I just want to sleep for hours and forget everything. Forget the video post, the amazing dates, Brad, Charlie, the drunken texts, and the nonexistent replies to them. I want to forget it all. But, of course, my mind won't let me.

I'll replay every moment, examine every word, every gesture, to see if I can pinpoint the exact moments that everything fell apart. Because, God damn it, it feels like everything is falling apart.

I don't like this feeling. At all.

Stop the world, I want to get off, please.

thirty-three
four letter words

Tess

I t's now Monday morning, and I still haven't heard anything from Brad. I didn't text him anymore, figuring I'd done enough damage on Saturday night. If he wanted to respond, he would have. I guess, he just didn't want to.

Every time I think that thought, my heart sinks lower. I've been in a tailspin since yesterday, and instead of sleeping off my hangover like I wanted to, I spent the day chasing my tail of twisted internal narratives. I read and reread my wall of texts to Brad, and nothing relationship-shattering jumped out at me. Was I annoying? Absolutely. Did it warrant a complete brush-off? I don't think so.

But then, maybe I don't know Brad like I thought I did. That's the main thing that jumps into the forefront of my brain. I thought we did, but maybe we don't know each other well enough to really know anything. Especially about how each of us handles stuff like this. Maybe this is normal.

I don't like this normal.

I get to the practice space super early. I'm not able to sleep anyway, so I may as well get a jump start on the workday. Getting ahead of the week's social media plans and website updates is a perfect way to distract me from my love life, or lack thereof. I clutch my coffee cup to warm my hands from the chilly air of the large space and hunker down into PR mode.

"There you are," Charlie's exuberant voice pulls me out of my tunnel vision focus. I look up to find her barreling toward me, arms open wide for a hug. On impact, she nearly knocks me over, and I barely have time to react to what's happening.

She squeezes her arms around my neck, making me choke out laughter. This is what I needed today, and I didn't even know it.

"Hey, Charlie, what's up?" I ask, hugging her back. She's still got my neck in a chokehold and doesn't seem inclined to let go any time soon. In fact, she starts rocking from side to side to drag the hug out even longer. I'm not sure what to make of any of this.

I glance up to find Brad watching us, but his face is completely blank and void of all emotions. My smile falters as our eyes meet. There's usually a spark of something behind those beautiful gray eyes, even if it's negative – his eyes always give away his emotions. But not now. There's not even an inkling of anger, or disdain.

"Hey," I say to him, prying Charlie off me, and forcing the smile back that had begun to wane for her benefit.

"I guess we're the early birds, huh?" he finally says, sitting on the chair across from me. I mentally note that he chose not to sit next to me on the couch, where there is plenty of room. The bad feeling in my gut increases as I watch him look at his phone instead of at me.

"Today, I'm gonna have us make butterfly wings that we can wear," Charlie announces, grabbing a bag full of craft supplies from near Brad. "I've got it all planned out, and the girls are going to love it. No peeking until we're done."

"You got it," Brad says, still engrossed in his phone. "No looking."

"I can't wait to see them," I say as she goes, the enthusiasm weak in my voice, but wanting to encourage her. I know how hard she plans their crafting projects. She's going to make a great manager of some kind one day.

Once she starts getting settled in the corner, and I'm pretty sure she can't hear what we're saying, I turn to Brad. "Is everything okay? I didn't hear from you yesterday."

He nods, still focused on his phone. "Yeah, everything's great. Sorry we got busy shopping for butterfly stuff yesterday. It must have slipped my mind."

His knee starts bouncing like he's nervous about something, and my stomach clenches even more. It slipped his mind? He's not thinking about me twenty-four seven like I'm thinking about him. It's not fair to expect that kind of concentration on me, but not even a passing thought?

Ouch.

"Sorry about all the drunk texts on Saturday. Ivy and I got a little bit carried away..." The heat on my face from embarrassment doesn't even matter because he doesn't even glance my way.

Instead, he shrugs. *He fucking shrugs.*

"S'cool. Happens to the best of us. No worries."

That's it. I can't take anymore.

"Is something wrong?" I ask, not liking the vibe I'm getting from him at all. It's not like him to brush me off like this, or anyone. Brad isn't the kind of guy to ignore things, or people. It's just not his nature. Everyone can get distracted, sure, but this is over the top.

Finally, he runs a hand through his hair and meets my eyes, and I don't like what I see. Apprehension. He's holding back something, and I can't tell what it is.

"No babe, everything's fine. I had a bit too much fun Saturday night myself, and just got busy yesterday with Charlie once she got home. That's all." His lips curve into a smile that makes his face light up. The knot in my stomach loosens, and I smile back, a sense of relief washing over me.

I need to get out of my head and stop overthinking everything. If left to my own devices, I'll doom us both without a word being spoken. My mind can be a terrible place to live once doubts start taking residence. I've sabotaged relationships by not being able to trust. I don't want that to happen with Brad. I want to believe that he means what he says.

The door swings open and Hayley and June come storming in with a haggard Ian trailing behind. It looks like the weekend took something out of all of us. Except the kids, of course. The girls start hopping in a circle with excitement, reminiscing about their amusement park trip. I want to grab some of that emotion and bottle it for myself. If anything, it's a distraction from the awkwardness between me and Brad. And that is something I can definitely use.

Just moments later, Emmett and Stefan arrive, and Dakota follows not long after. The room is once again filled with music as the guys work through their set for a string of upcoming shows around the southwest.

I've been busy with the promotional materials and social media surrounding the mini-tour and keeping tabs with Eliza and Ian to monitor ticket sales. All but two shows are already sold out, and we've been in discussions with venues to possibly add more dates. Things are moving fast, now that Dakota has found his place in the band, and everyone is clicking on all cylinders.

During their rehearsal, every now and then, I look up to watch the guys play and I'll catch Brad looking at me. We'll lock eyes and I'll get warm all over. As he holds the mic, I'll remember what his hands felt like on my bare skin, and as he sings, I can picture his lips all over me. I find myself blushing almost every time our eyes meet, and when I do, he smiles at me, probably thinking the same exact things I am.

"It's going well, yeah?" Ian asks, sitting next to me on the couch to watch the rehearsal. He's been bouncing around like a pinball between the guys, the girls, and various phone calls, but he's got everything under control. You would think the transition from rocker to music executive, to now band manager would be difficult, but he knows his shit, that's for sure. Experience in the different worlds helps.

"Yeah, and it looks like the new date in Phoenix is finalized, too," I say, showing him the email I just got from Eliza.

"Good, good. It's a great start."

I arch an eyebrow at him. "Start?"

He shrugs. "World domination. That's the goal, right? Get these guys in front of as many fans as possible. We're touring *one* corner of *one* country and look at the response. I think we're ready for more, don't you?"

Considering how well ticket sales are going, he might not be far off. But still, I'm apprehensive. Maybe because I'm still new to this I want to test the waters first. I can't help but feed off his positive attitude, though. He obviously knows what he's talking about.

"I'm still in research mode, but can't argue with the numbers so far," I say, raising my voice a little to be heard over the music. It might be my imagination, but it seems like they've turned up the volume at least a few levels.

During a break in the music, Brad's phone rings, and after looking at the screen, he excuses himself and steps outside. "I gotta take this guys. I'll be right back."

Ian and I take advantage of the relative quiet to call Eliza to discuss adding more dates to the tour. While they talk numbers and budgets, my mind wanders to Brad outside and his phone call. I know that Ren has been checking in a lot on Charlie, especially since the whole social media incident. She usually calls around this time of day, so I don't think too much about it. The rest of the band head out not long after for a smoke break.

After a few minutes, and the additional dates agreed on, Ian and I head outside to tell the guys the news. The bright sun is blinding at first, but once my eyes adjust, I notice Brad away from the rest, leaning against the building with his back to us, obviously on a video call.

"Well, I just wanted to say hi. I miss you so much. And I still care about you..." It's a female voice, and it's not Ren. My breath freezes in my lungs. Even Ian next to me halts in his tracks, unsure what to do.

"I still care about you too, babe..." Brad says without missing a beat. He didn't even have to think about it.

"Why don't we go inside, and we can talk to everyone after the break?" Ian suggests, grabbing my elbow gently and steering me back into the building. Emmett, Stefan, and Dakota all avoid meeting my eyes as we go, obviously embarrassed for me.

And that's what I am – embarrassed. It's the only thing I can even feel. I've been played like the fool that I am, and everyone here knows it. Shock doesn't even begin to cover it. I'm absolutely paralyzed emotionally.

There are no tears.

There's nothing.

I feel nothing.

As Ian ushers me toward the battered leather couch, the girls run up and start dancing around us. Their butterfly wings are complete, and they're showing them off. My brain is having a hard time switching gears from the utter devastation I'm feeling to the happy cacophony around me.

The wings really are beautiful, though, and I somehow find the strength to allow myself to be pulled into their excitement. These precious girls didn't hurt me. Charlie didn't betray me. Her father did, and I can't blame her for that.

"These are amazing, girls. You really outdid yourselves this time," I say, my throat tightening. Every ounce of energy I possess is being poured into keeping it together. A smile is a bit much to ask for, but I think I succeed in at least being earnest. The girls are too busy giggling and pretending to fly around to really notice anyway.

My heart hurts for Charlie too. I've really been growing close with her these last few weeks and can't stand the thought of disappointing her. I know what that's like, since I've been there too. Wanting a family; to see your parents happy and whole. To feel like you're a part of something bigger even though you don't quite understand it. I don't want to be the cause of her pain, even if it's not my fault.

When the guys come back in a few minutes later, Brad is still not with them. Meaning, he's probably still on the phone with whoever it was that 'misses him so much.' My heart clenches even more, though I'm still numb.

The awkwardness in the room could be cut with a knife, and I hate it. I hate being the center of attention, and even though everyone is purposely not looking at me, I know that I am what everyone is thinking about. They all know that I'm an idiot, and they also know that I just figured that out. If I was embarrassed a few minutes ago, it's only magnified exponentially now.

The only thing I can do is busy myself with my work, though I'm not really seeing the screen in front of me. Words are jumbling together, and pictures are unfocused. The layout for the latest graphic I was working on suddenly doesn't make sense to me. Nothing does.

Brad comes back, and I can't help but look up at him. Like a magnet, I'm still drawn to his every move. I can't help myself. Even now.

More like a moth to a flame, I think.

He gives me a smile and a wink as he walks past, and even touches my shoulder lightly. I instantly tense up, and my skin flares where his fingers grazed me, but I force myself not to react in any way. For some reason I don't want to give away that I overheard his conversation, and I don't know why.

"I still care about you too, babe..."

Part of me wants to scream at him right here and now in front of everyone, including Charlie, and another part wants to run away and hide, never to be found. All these instincts inside of me are warring with each other, and I can do nothing. My brain is still processing, and my heart is still breaking into a million tiny pieces. Each beat of my heart sends another jagged shard through my bloodstream, slicing at me and reminding me of the pain that's going to overtake me when I'm finally alone.

Ian reaches over and rubs my shoulder gently for a moment, and that little act of kindness almost undoes me. It's sympathy, and I appreciate it, but it's too much. I was fine until this moment, though that's probably a lie, too.

The unshed tears are burning behind my eyes, and my throat hurts as I hold in the scream that wants to let loose. I can't be here anymore.

"I need to go," I say roughly to Ian, gathering my things as the band starts into their set again. I grab my purse and laptop, and wave goodbye to the girls. "I'll keep up with our group chat on the new dates, okay?" I say to Ian, not waiting for his response.

I push through the door and hurry to my car, on the brink of losing it. Somehow, I make it behind the wheel before the tears break free. And once they start, I don't think they'll ever stop.

I hate myself for letting this happen. I knew better than to get involved with someone like Brad. I knew his history. I knew his reputation, and yet somehow, I thought he'd change for me? I'm *that* special that I can change someone's innate way of being? Please. I'm not special at all. Brad's proven that hasn't he?

Alarm bells were going off in my head, and I just started dancing along, ignoring their dire warning to pay attention. To run away. To do the right thing and protect myself.

Well, I get it now. Too late, but I get it.

The damage, however, is already done.

thirty-four
life support

Brad

When Tess leaves in a hurry after we start back into our set, I wonder what the rush is about, but nobody seems too phased by it. And when Ian tells us that we're adding dates to the tour, it kind of makes sense why she would make a quick exit. She's probably on her way to Blackmore to meet with Eliza to go over the media plan for everything.

However, by the end of rehearsal, I get the distinct feeling that something is off with everyone. Practice went fine, but it's almost like everyone is avoiding me, or mad at me, and I have no idea why.

"So, what's up with everyone?" I finally ask, as Ian leaves with his daughters. Charlie's in the corner cleaning up, so she's out of earshot if there is a problem I need to deal with. "Why is there a stick up everyone's ass all of a sudden?"

Stefan eyes me with a shrug as he winds up a cord. "Nothing, man. Just same old, same old."

Emmett and Dakota regard him briefly, then seem to accept his answer as their own, going back to what they were doing. Apparently, there is nothing wrong, and it's all in my head. With the new dates added, and ticket sales going so well, I'd expect at least a little more enthusiasm from these guys. That alone makes me wonder if Stefan is telling the truth.

I study everyone again, looking for whatever it is that I'm obviously missing, but Charlie comes running up behind me and hugs my leg.

"Can we go now Daddy?" she asks, turning her face up to me, her innocent eyes wide. I know spending so much time here wasn't her idea of fun when she chose to stay with me. If Hayley and June weren't here to keep her company all the time, she'd be regretting her choice.

"Sure thing," I say, ruffling her curls. I grab her hand to leave and turn back to the guys. "Catch you all tomorrow."

They all wave and mumble their goodbyes, mostly to Charlie than to me. That's fine. I don't need the niceties, and Charlie beams at them as she flounces next to me, her newly crafted butterfly wings flapping behind her. They really are beautiful, but they've taken a beating this afternoon with all of her running around and are looking a little worse for wear. She sure loves hard.

Just like her dad.

In the car on the way home, the questions start. And they don't stop.

"Can we have dinner with Tess tonight?"

"Probably not tonight. Tess is pretty busy with our upcoming tour, babe."

"What about tomorrow night? Will she be busy then?"

"Maybe. We'll have to ask her."

"Can you call her now and ask?"

"No. I'm driving."

"But you always talk to people when you drive."

"Only if they call me and it's important."

"Isn't dinner with Tess important?"

"Of course it is."

"Then you should call her."

And on it goes for the half hour it takes to get food and get home. I've tried to beat down Charlie's expectations as delicately and diplomatically as possible, but she's persistent. Just as I thought my feelings for Tess were solidifying, I got the definite sense that something was off today. Throw in my ex Sierra's fucking weird phone call out of nowhere this afternoon, which only confirmed how I feel about Tess, and now I feel a little lost. I don't want Charlie to get hurt by whatever might be going on.

I've been thinking about Tess nonstop since we met, and the last few days have been a bit of an emotional rollercoaster already. And now, everything feels like it's out of whack.

"You should call Tess and see if she wants to go to dinner tomorrow," Charlie pipes in again, breaking my train of thought.

I roll my eyes and sigh dramatically. This kid. "Fine.

But I'll text her. If she's busy, I don't want to bug her. Deal?"

She rolls her eyes and sighs right back at me. Man, we are too alike sometimes. "*Fiiine.*"

I grab my phone to type out a quick text message, noticing all of Tess's drunk texts from Saturday night. They really are cute. If I weren't too drunk myself on Saturday night to notice them, it could have been an oddly sweet moment – the two of us drunk texting each other from across the city.

Instead, I was too hungover to deal with them when I did notice them yesterday, and too wrapped up in all things Charlie shopping for school supplies and butterfly parts the rest of the day to respond. Maybe that was a misstep?

ME: Hey there. Dinner sometime this week if you're not too busy?

After a few minutes, Charlie asks, "Well? What did she say?"

I know there hasn't been a response, but I glance at my phone to check anyway. Nothing.

"I told you she's probably busy," I say, looking around the room for something, *anything*, to distract Charlie from this. Hell, to distract *me* from this. We've both got our hopes up, and there's a sinking feeling in my gut that we're both about to be severely disappointed. "How about we watch a movie? We haven't ripped apart the new Lion King in a while..."

As we watch the movie, in our usual spots on the couch, popcorn bowl between us, I can't help but drift my gaze to my phone every few minutes, willing it to light up with an alert from Tess. The longer time drags on without a response, the more I know that something's wrong. But what could it be?

Is it because I didn't respond to her texts over the weekend? I think Tess would understand that when I'm with Charlie, I'm not always tied to my phone. At least I would hope that's the case. I'm pretty sure Tess and Charlie have formed a mutual admiration society for each other. At least, for Charlie's sake, I hope that Tess feels the same for her. I'm biased and think everyone should love my little girl like I do, though. So, there's that.

However, knowing how past girlfriends have used Charlie and her affections to get to me, makes me rethink everything. Are we too far in to avoid that heartache already?

Am *I* that far gone?

I glance at my silent phone one more time.

Still nothing.

thirty-five
shame on me

Tess

My phone dings with another text alert from Brad, and I just turn off notifications. Now I know how he felt over the weekend with my incessant stupid texts. This is different, though.

Very different.

I've been crying since I left the studio, and I can't seem to stop the tears. I really did let myself fall for Brad and think that I was somehow special to him. I opened myself up for this pain, knowing his reputation, hell – even running into one of his exes on our first damned date.

Hello? Red flag.

I should have known better. I'm not rockstar-girl-friend material. My skin isn't thick enough. I don't have the emotional fortitude to deal with this kind of thing. I have enough trust issues thanks to my past relationships to know that much. I'm not strong enough to let things go so quickly. When I hurt, I hold it close.

Did he really think I wouldn't find out he still has feelings for someone else? Does he really think that little of me? Hell, if he was just honest about it from the beginning I could possibly understand. Lingering emotions for exes are normal – it's what you do with them that matters. Discussing those feelings with your ex and hiding it from your current love interest is not how you deal with that. Not in any universe I'm aware of, at least.

Honesty and clear communication are so crucial, especially in a new relationship. The disrespect I should be feeling, however, is dwarfed by the overwhelming hurt that is drowning me. It's only been a few weeks, and I've fallen so hard for Brad so quickly, I should have known that it was too good to be true.

My phone lights up, and I can't help but look to see if it's another text or call from Brad, but it's Ivy.

Shit.

Do I want to tell this story yet? Share this pain with my best friend? Or do I still want to hold onto it a little longer and dwell in my sorrow alone? I give in and answer, not hiding the fact that I've been crying.

"Hello?" I croak, my throat raw with emotion.

"How are you holding up?" she asks, sympathy in her voice. That throws me off kilter.

"How do you know what happened?" There's no way Ivy could possibly know what happened this afternoon.

She hesitates. "What do you mean? It's all over the internet."

A lump forms in my throat, nearly choking me, and my heart starts racing. The entire world now knows my shame and betrayal. What the hell?

"How? Nobody else was there..."

"Wait. What?" she sounds just as confused as I do. "Where?"

We're getting nowhere fast with this kind of questioning.

"How about you tell me what you're talking about," I offer, trying to calm my breathing that's running away with me.

"The story about Brad and his ex, Sienna something-or-other, getting back together. She just did a tell-all with *Blindsided*, and the internet is eating it up."

"Sierra," I correct, going through the rolodex of ex-girlfriends in my head. Of course, I know who all of his exes are, it was part of my research for the band when I took the PR job. I had to know everything about who or what could pop out of the woodwork, and here she is.

That must be who Brad was talking to earlier today. Sierra Stevens, the swimsuit model from Texas, where things are definitely...bigger. They were on-and-off with each other for a year or so before he got together with Gina. And if I remember correctly, they were even engaged at one point. She's the only one that got that close with him.

Of course, she is. She's perfect. She was a bit of a media darling for a while, so I'm not at all surprised that she's gone to the tabloids with this story.

"Is it true?" Ivy asks, and the reality of it hits me like a ton of bricks.

The tears start again, and no matter how hard I try, I can't hold them back. I'm such an idiot.

"I think so."

"What does that mean? You *think* so? Didn't Brad say anything?"

'I still care about you too, babe...'

Those words still ricochet around my heart, bruising everything in their path.

"Not directly, but I overheard a conversation earlier between the two of them that would confirm it." Saying it out loud should make me feel better, but instead I feel even more like shit.

"Oh," Ivy says quietly, but then shifts gears. "Well then, fuck that guy. He doesn't deserve you anyway."

"Ivy..."

"I mean it. You are a fucking Goddess, and he should feel honored to even be in your presence. If he's too blind to see that, then fuck him."

I appreciate what she's trying to do, I really do, but it's too much. I need to withdraw for a minute. Take a breath. But the world has other ideas about what I need, apparently.

The call is interrupted by another one. Eliza.

"I have to go, Ivy. Work is calling," I say, trying to steel myself for the upcoming onslaught that I need to put my professional hat on for, even though my heart is still breaking.

"Okay but call me back. Don't shut down. Got it?"

"Got it," I say, and take a deep breath before switching calls, the tremor in my voice thankfully gone for the time being. "Hi Eliza."

"I take it you've seen the *Blindsided* article?" she asks, and I detect an edge of worry in her tone.

"I literally just heard about it, and am now looking into it..." It's the truth at least. Not all of it, but it's all Eliza needs to know.

"Well, talk to Brad, and get his side of it. If it's true, fine. Whatever. We'll deal with it. But if it's not, we need to shut it down. We can't have people using Chaos Fuel's rising star to pull themselves up. You know what I mean?"

The thought of confronting Brad about this makes me feel sick to my stomach. That's the last thing I want to do right now. But, of course, it's also my job.

"I understand," I say, determined to keep things professional. "I'm on it. Don't worry."

"Okay. Do your thing, Tess."

We end the call, and I stare at my phone blankly. I don't want to do this.

I could quit. Find work somewhere else. Anywhere else. I could move to another country and do *any* other kind of job. One that doesn't deal with people. One that doesn't rip my heart to shreds. Or I could go back to fixing politician's fucked up lives... That thought turns my stomach.

The runaway train that is my thought process derails, and I think about Charlie. The little girl with the big brain and even bigger heart. She tried so hard to get me and her dad together, I don't know how she's going to react to him and Sierra. Does Sierra care about Charlie like I do? Does she play games and do crafts with her? Talk to her like she's a real person and not just a child?

I'm losing so much more than Brad, and the magnitude of it is killing me. If I'm honest with myself, I did let my imagination run a little wild with the idea of us all together. Even if it was only part-time with Charlie, it felt like we had created a wonderful dynamic between the three of us. We were forging bonds I didn't even know existed, or only dreamt of.

And now...

thirty-six
lost in echoes

Brad

O ut of nowhere, my phone starts blowing up. My first thought, well, hope, is that it's Tess, and I jump to answer it, only to find that it's Ian.

"Just a head's up that your secret is out," Ian announces, not even a *'hello,'* or, *'how are you?'* to start the conversation politely. That's not like him.

"Secret? What secret?" I glance over at Charlie, half-asleep on the couch next to me, and make my way to my bedroom down the hall. That initial statement makes me think this is going to be a crazy discussion. I am not wrong.

"About you and Sierra," he adds, sounding disappointed.

I may not be disappointed currently, but I'm sure as fuck confused.

"Me and Sierra? What the fuck are you talking about?"

"Don't act so surprised, Brad. She went to the

tabloids and told them you're back together." He hesitates for a second, and with a sigh says, "And, Tess and I overheard your conversation with her earlier today, so the cat's out of the bag. But why is she going to the press with this stuff? Did you guys think it would help—"

"What the *fuck* are you talking about?" I shout, disbelief clouding my vision momentarily. I literally have to blink several times to focus on anything again. "Sierra and I are *not* back together. And we won't ever be."

"Well, that's not what she told *Blindsided*."

"I don't give a shit what she told anyone; it's not fucking true." My heart is about to pound out of my chest, and I start pacing around the bed, trying to make sense of what he's saying. I can hear other phone notifications trying to break through the call, but I ignore them for now. I need to know what the fuck is happening.

"She said, and I quote, *'Brad and I realized during our time apart that we were made for each other. No matter how much we tried to forget the other person and move on, we just couldn't. We were meant to be...'"*

"What the actual fuck?" I growl, my teeth and fists now clenching. There was no indication whatsoever during my call with Sierra that she would do something like this. She *tried* to get back together with me, but it didn't work. I shot her down as gently as I could. Even though we broke up because of her lying to the press about a supposed 'engagement' that never happened, I never hated her. Shit, I still considered us friends after the call this afternoon. Well, fuck that now. She just burned that bridge with napalm.

I rake an angry hand through my hair, grabbing a fistful and debating pulling it out by the roots. I don't know that I've ever been this mad before in my life. And to be fair, I've had a lot of fucked up shit happen to me.

Charlie's small voice from the doorway freezes me in place.

"Daddy? What's wrong?"

Fuck. Fuck. Fuck.

"I'll call you back," I mumble to Ian before hanging up the call.

I don't want to turn around. I don't want to see the anxiety and confusion on my baby girl's face. And I sure as shit don't want to explain what the fuck is going on right now.

But I can't lie to her either. That's not how we do things.

My phone starts ringing again, and I see that it's Tess. My heart lurches, wanting to take the call and explain myself, but I need to explain this to Charlie first. She's my priority. Always.

Switching my phone off, I fall onto the edge of my bed, patting the space next to me for her to sit with me. She hesitates at first, wary of my sour mood, but jumps up and leans her head onto my arm.

"What happened?" she asks quietly.

Jesus. Where do I begin? Sierra was one of the few girlfriends that I had that got along with Charlie. At least, I thought they did. Maybe that was all a lie too. Then again, I was still in and out of parenthood at the time, and they really didn't see all that much of each other.

"Do you remember Sierra?"

"Yeah. She was pretty."

Charlie was around five when Sierra and I dated, so maybe her memory of her isn't as solid as I'd thought. That could turn out to be a saving grace if she's not expecting much from her.

"She was. Well, she's telling people that she and I are back together..."

Charlie sits up straight, automatic defiance taking her small frame over. I see so much of myself in her right now. "But you're with Tess. Not Sierra. She's lying."

I nod. "She is lying." Memories of Tess leaving today's rehearsal in a hurry come crashing into my mind. That's why she left so quickly. What did Ian say? They overheard my conversation? Well, part of it anyway. They obviously didn't hear the whole thing. Now it all makes sense. "And I think Tess might think Sierra is telling the truth."

"But, why?" Charlie's brow furrows, and her confusion is so relatable, but at the same time it strikes a chord of guilt through me.

I replay everything that I said to Sierra this afternoon, and for the life of me, I can't imagine what they overheard to make her believe any of this. But Tess is no fool. There must have been something that triggered her. I've obviously done something to fuck things up.

"I'm not entirely sure, but I'm going to call her now

and try to clear this up." It's the best I can do. I can't promise anything. "Give me a few minutes?"

She hugs me tightly, which is exactly what I need in this moment, and then slides off the bed. "Make sure you tell Tess that you love her, so that she can tell you're telling the truth."

My brows raise. "Love her? It's a bit soon, don't you think?" Am I considering dating advice from my eight-year-old? I think I am. But love? Really? Is that what we're talking about?

She stops in the doorway, and glances back at me over her shoulder. "But it's the truth, isn't it? You love her?"

She disappears back down the hall before I can answer, let alone think of one.

Way to hit and run little one.

thirty-seven
true colors

Tess

He doesn't answer. I finally got the nerve up to call and face whatever is going on, and he doesn't even answer. Of course he doesn't. He's probably trying to avoid me at all costs, just like earlier at rehearsals. What else did I expect? For him to just come out and admit that he's been stringing me along this whole time?

People don't work that way. Especially rockstars. He's probably got 'girlfriends' in every damn town they've ever played for all I know. Sierra is just the tip of the iceberg. There are plenty more where she came from, I'm sure. Guys like Brad don't stick to just one person. They can't. It's not in their nature.

Eliza's call had bolstered me into action. Be professional. Do my fucking job. Get the details. Spin it in whatever way is best for the band. For the label. For Brad.

But what about me? Where do I fit into any of this? Other than the one doing the clean up? How can I clean up a mess that has utterly destroyed me, only minutes after it happened?

All my life I have had to be the strong one. The one who fixes things. From my family to my friends, to my love life. It's what I do, and I do it well, which is why this profession is perfect for me. But this is going above and beyond.

Being the strong one all the time is exhausting. I'm tested repeatedly, just to see how well I can take the hit, and I'm tired. Tired of getting back up and dusting myself off, only to be decimated again. Tired of being the person who isn't supposed to react. Take it on the chin and ask for more.

I don't want any more.

I want to be the person being supported. Held together. Cared for. Thought about. Just once, I want to know what that feels like. Sure, I'd probably freak the fuck out about it because it would be so foreign, but I still want it. I yearn for it. My entire being craves it.

But like everything else coming to light today, I know deep down that I'll never have that. It's not in my cards to be able to let my guard down and let someone in. I was beginning to think that maybe Brad was someone I could do that with. Boy, was I wrong. I'll just need to relearn how to live with that.

The phone vibrates in my hands, making me jump, and tearing me out of my inner downward spiral.

It's Brad.

You can do this. You can do this.

"Hey, Brad."

Professional. I'm a professional.

"Hey…Tess," he stutters, probably caught off guard by my nonchalant tone.

Good. Be off balance. Asshole.

I jump in before he can start with his excuses. "I called a little while ago because Eliza wants me to solidify the story that Sierra gave to *Blindsided*. We can start using it for publicity on the upcoming tour and maybe even add dates in Texas where she's from. You know, do the whole 'hometown' thing? Do you have any recent pictures of you two together I can use for posts? I'd like to start working on that first thing tomorrow if you—"

"Sierra and I are not together," he interrupts my long-winded diatribe.

I'm not sure I heard him correctly. "But the article—"

"Is complete bullshit. She made it up." I can sense his anger just from his tone of voice, but it's still *off*.

"Okay…" This doesn't make any sense, and now I'm getting angry again. Does he really think I'm that stupid? "But I heard you talking to her earlier outside of rehearsal. I heard what you said, Brad."

"What, exactly, did you hear me say, Tess? What were my exact fucking words?"

Is he actually mad at me about this? Like I did something wrong here? Oh no. He's got another thing coming if that's the case.

"Are you trying to turn this around on me right now?

Because that's not how this works. I am talking to you as the PR person for Blackmore Records, assigned to your band to fix your image. Nothing more."

"No...fuck. Of course I'm not blaming you." He's quiet for a long moment, and I can almost hear him pacing. "I'm trying to figure out what you heard that would make you think I'd go back with Sierra, that's all. Because that was not how the conversation actually went."

"Oh, really?" I can't keep the shock out of my voice. "Because I heard, *'I still care about you too, babe...'* clear as fucking day. And I'm not the only one. Actually, everyone outside at the time heard it. It was lovely. Fucking embarrassing as all get out, but absolutely beautiful. I'm happy for you. Truly, I am."

"Tess, you didn't hear the rest of it."

"Oh, there was more? Gee, I'm so sorry I missed it." My sarcasm is taking over, and I can't help but let it loose. I'm hurting, and my first instinct is to hurt back. "I'm sure it was absolutely enlightening."

"Tess..."

"No, please. Go on. I want to hear everything about the star-crossed lovers, who still care about each other so much after all this time. The pair who are, what did she call it? *'Meant to be?'* That's it. Tell me that story. You're good at stories, too. Right, Brad? Isn't that all you've been telling me? Stories? First Gina on our first date, and now this?"

"That's not fair, and you know it."

"Oh, I'm aware that nothing's fair. Believe me, I'm well aware of that fact."

He lets out a long breath. "I can't do this..."

And the line goes dead.

He hung up on me.

Brad fucking Chambers just hung up on me.

thirty-eight
i'd rather see your star explode

Brad

I'm gripping the phone in my hand so tightly; I think I might crush it with my fist. Actually, I wouldn't mind too much if I broke it. All it's doing is causing destruction.

I can't believe this is happening.

Why in the world did Sierra do this? What is she getting out of this? When I talked to her earlier, I was crystal clear that we weren't getting back together. I haven't even read the article about it yet, but I don't need to. The fallout from it tells me all I need to know.

And from Tess's reaction, I know that she's hurting. I didn't do a God damned thing but answer a phone call, and now my life is in utter shambles.

I need to fix this. But how? What the fuck can I do from here to fix anything? My mind races, searching for a solution to this cluster fuck, and how I can convince Tess that I'm telling her the truth.

Fuck it. I need to talk to Tess face to face. She needs to see for herself that I mean what I say.

I call Ian and explain the situation as best as I can while packing Charlie's overnight bag. He agrees to take her for the night for an impromptu sleepover so that I can go to Tess's and explain in person. This isn't something that can be resolved over the phone.

Charlie is surprised, but excited at the change in plans. However, she's feeding off my energy, and can tell that things still aren't right.

"You're going to talk to Tess?" she asks, holding my hand as we head to the car.

"I am," I say, again not wanting to get her hopes up that I'll be able to fix anything. At the moment, my failure in that department is pretty apparent.

"Good. Well, tell her that Sierra lied. That should fix it."

"I'll do what I can baby girl, but Tess is pretty hurt by everything. I don't know if that will fix it."

"Then tell her you're sorry. If you apologize, it'll be okay."

God, I wish it was that easy. That cut and dry. That fucking simple.

"We'll see." It's as definitive as I can get right now. I don't know how this is going to go, and to be honest, I'm scared.

When Tess opens the door to her apartment and finds me on the other side, the hurt in her eyes that she's trying desperately not to show nearly kills me. Guilt rolls through me, even though I know in my heart that I've done nothing wrong. I would never purposely do anything to hurt Tess, but somehow, I found a way to do it without even trying.

Even in her disheveled state, she's beautiful. Her hair up in a messy bun, an oversized t-shirt and sweatpants, and her arms around her waist, hugging herself. I want so badly to pull her into my arms and never let go, but I know that's the wrong move. Her eyes are wary when they finally meet mine.

"What are you doing here?" she asks, shifting her gaze to the ground between us.

I shuffle my feet uncomfortably. "We obviously need to talk."

"We were talking. You hung up on me." Her chin juts out, and her shoulders straighten as her eyes lift to mine again with defiance. "I'd say the window for discussion is now closed."

Swallowing hard, I'm not going to let it end like this. Not with her thinking I would do this to her. "I'm sorry about that. I didn't mean to hang up on you. I was just so...*fucking* frustrated. You have no idea how twisted this whole thing has become. Please, just let me explain my side."

Her cold eyes study me, and I can feel the chill on my skin. It cuts through me.

She debates turning me away, but then says, "Fine," as she steps aside to let me in.

Good. I'm in the door at least. I didn't think I'd even get this far.

I stand in the middle of the living room awkwardly, memories of our time together here just the other day. It's a complete mind fuck that things have changed so much in such a short period of time. And all because of something out of our control. All because someone else wants to fuck with me.

Tess sits in the solo armchair, pulling her knees up and hugging them, a clear sign that she doesn't want me near her. I move to the end of the couch closest to her, pushing aside thoughts of how I held her right here in this spot on Friday night.

On the way over, I tried to think of words that would fix this. Charlie's simple suggestions bounced around, and while seemingly oversimplified, they do cut right to the heart of things.

"I'm sorry," I say, trying to convey the absolute truth of it. "I'm sorry this is happening. And I'm sorry that it's affecting you. But Tess, you have to believe me – I am not back with Sierra. I don't know why she said what she did, but you didn't hear the entire conversation."

Her face is completely blank. No emotion whatsoever. She looks so fucking tired and drained. I hate that this is doing this to her. She doesn't respond but turns her flat gaze to me. I take that as encouragement to continue.

"You heard me tell her that I still cared about her,

and I do. That's true. I care on some level for everyone I've been involved with. But like I told her, I'm not *in love* with her. I don't know if I ever was. And I was crystal clear with her that I was with someone else."

I pause, waiting for some kind of reaction, but there is none. She's still staring at me, studying me, looking for a crack. Looking for the lie.

"That's the truth, Tess. I swear."

"Why would she say it, then?" her voice wavers, and I can tell she's holding back tears. I want to jump over and pull her to me. Console her. Make all her pain go away. But I see the doubt behind all her pain. She's lost whatever faith she had in me.

"I don't know," I shrug. Why does anyone do shit like this? Sierra never seemed the type to chase fame like this, but then, people do desperate things. I just never expected her to use me to do it. "Please believe me. I'm with you. Nobody else."

Her expression softens just the slightest bit, and my heart leaps at the thought that maybe things will be okay between us. Maybe she hasn't given up on me entirely. I really don't know what I'll do if she has.

Tess's phone starts dinging with notifications, and mine follows just a moment later. Our eyes meet, and the fear I see in hers devastates me. Neither of us wants to look at our phones. The sinking feeling in my gut that whatever this news is will be the final straw.

Eventually we both give in and look at our phones. There's a message from Ian with a link to another *Blindsided* article. The headline makes my blood run ice cold.

'Hands Off My Baby Daddy.' – *Gina Winston, former Chaos Fuel frontman Brad Chambers' flame, claims they're building a family, contradicting Sierra Stevens' latest story of reconciliation.*

I put my phone away and drop my face into my hands. What the fuck is going on? And what the fuck am I doing? Thinking that I could drag Tess into this nightmare. She doesn't deserve this shit. And that's exactly what this is – bullshit.

She should be with someone whose past won't haunt them like this. In public. She didn't ask for this. In some twisted way, I did. When I became a singer in a band, I wanted fame. The recognition. I wanted the world to talk about me and my music. Maybe even a part of me wanted the 'Ladies Man' title. Once upon a time that was true. But not anymore.

Too bad, fuckhead. You asked for it. You got it. And now you need to live with it.

I do. But Tess shouldn't have to. I don't want to keep hurting her like this. Who knows who the fuck else is going to come crawling out of my past to drag me down, and Tess right along with me?

Wiping my hands down my face, I glance over to Tess. She's still reading, and she's gone pale. Her hands are shaking slightly, but her eyes are dry.

Dry and full of pain. And distrust.

Gina just poured kerosene on the inferno of lies surrounding me. Other people's lies – but ones that look like they're convincing Tess. She'll never believe me now. Nobody has before, so why would she?

It's more than evident – I've lost her.

I can feel my heart break, knowing that we could have had something special. Something I've longed for my entire life. But my fucked-up past is always going to come between us. It's always going to be a shadow over us, causing doubts and insecurities to seep into the corners of her mind about me. I don't want that for her. That's no way for her to live.

She deserves so much better.

"I'm so sorry, Tess," I say, making sure she meets my eyes and sees that truth. It's the only thing I can give her now. "I'm sorry you got caught in the middle of my bullshit."

I can't stand it, seeing her like this. I need to leave and let her be. She's got a PR shitstorm to deal with now, and it's all my fault – even though I didn't do a God damned thing, other than be nice to an ex. That'll teach me a lesson.

Note to self – just be a dick.

Well, fuck. I'm good at that.

Getting up from the couch, I head to the door before I change my mind and fall to my knees begging for her to take me back despite my past rearing its ugly head. Making sure not to meet her eyes and see the pain I know is there, I mumble, "Let me know if you need me to make a statement or something."

And I leave.

thirty-nine
said & done

Tess

I barely have time to register the latest scandal when Brad gets up and heads to the door to leave.

"Let me know if you need me to make a statement or something."

Jumping up from the chair, I don't know what I'm doing, but for some reason I don't want him to go. I run to the door and call after him, halfway to his car already. "Wait, you're just leaving?"

I'm not feeling a single emotion. I haven't had a chance to sort any of them out. Too much is happening way too fast.

He stops, his back stiffening, and his shoulders slump as his head lowers before he turns to face me. He's overcome by sadness, and it's painful to see.

"I can't do this," he says, his arms going limp at his sides. It's defeat. He's giving up.

So easily.

"Can't do what, Brad?" I ask, feeling the ground

open beneath my feet, ready to swallow me whole. My heart is finally catching up, and it doesn't like where this is headed.

"Can't keep hurting you." His eyes flash with anger, and I can tell it's directed at himself. He's taking the blame for all of this, but I'm starting to see that it's not his fault. I should have seen it before.

"Brad—"

"Tess, please. It's best for all of us if we just go back to being professionals. I can't be in a relationship with you while also expecting you to clean up shit like this. It's not fair."

"Oh, so, just shut up and do my job then, huh?" I cross my arms, now getting mad at him too. At least it's an emotion. "Is that what you're saying?"

"No, that's not what I'm fucking saying." He takes a step toward me but stops and runs his hands through his hair. The anguish in his tone is pulling at me. "For fuck's sake, can my words not get fucking twisted just once today? Jesus Christ."

I'm taken back by the venom in his words, and don't know how to react. This feels all wrong. I still can't wrap my head around anything that's happening, this isn't right.

"Then let me get this straight," I say, finding my backbone. "Your past crawls out of the woodwork, spews a bunch of bullshit that crushes my soul, and now you're breaking up with me because of it? Do I have that right?"

I can't believe this is happening.

He closes the distance between us and grabs my

upper arms. The intensity between us ratches up a notch, and the warmth of him so close makes me want to fight for this even harder. This should not be going this way. We should be working through this. Not giving up. I am so confused.

"I am no good for you, Tess. You've got to see that," he pleads, and my heart twists into knots. "Believe me, ending this now is best for both of us."

So, he is giving up. Just like that.

I stare up at him, trying to think of words that will change his mind, but I can see that anything I say will fall on deaf ears. He's made his mind up.

It's over.

He moves as if to pull me closer but stops himself. My entire body aches to lean into him; find comfort in the man that is causing my pain. It makes no sense, but I just want to stop time for one second, just to feel his arms around me one more time. One last moment of connection between us before I'm left alone again.

Gravity finally pulls every emotion from me when he lets go and walks back to his car without another word, leaving me empty. The evening chill sinks deeper into my bones.

"Please don't do this," I say flatly, but it's too low for him to hear. Or if he does hear, he ignores it.

I force myself to watch as he pulls away, taking all my dreams with him as he goes.

In the blink of any eye, the beat of two hearts, everything I ever wanted crumbles into dust.

Just like that.

forty
like i do

Brad

I had to do it. Didn't I?

The only way to protect Tess, and even Charlie, is to keep them out of everything related to me. It's why I keep Charlie out of the press. To keep the vultures from feeding on her life. It's *her* life, not the public's.

The same applies to Tess.

This way she can have a normal life, whatever that fucking means. She can keep her personal life private – with whoever she ends up with. Whoever can love her the way she deserves to be loved.

Whoever isn't me.

When I get home, I collapse onto the couch, my body and mind numb. I've been so busy considering Tess and Charlie, that I haven't even thought about myself in all this.

First, Sierra going completely off the rails and saying that we're back together out of nowhere. Where the fuck did that come from? She never gave a single sign that she'd do something like that.

And then Gina – what the fuck is that even about? I didn't take the time to even read that bullshit. I don't have the mental bandwidth to even try to figure that out.

Gina's always been one to play mind games. Hot one minute and cold the next. It was a rollercoaster I never wanted to be on, but there were moments that I thought made it worth the ride. Same with Sierra. There were glimmers of light that I thought outshone the dark times between us, but they were just flickers. Neither of them comes remotely close to how I feel when I'm with Tess.

Fuck, even when I'm not with her.

Even now, when I know I've just ended the best thing that ever happened to me, just the thought of her being happy – even with somebody else - fills me up with emotions I can't put a name to. Yes, I've broken us apart, but I've also set her free. She's free from this bullshit world of constant turmoil that surrounds me day and night.

She's free of me.

Charlie's sweet face fills my mind. She's going to be devastated at what I've done. She won't understand. Explaining to an eight-year-old that the world is a cruel place, and I'm just trying to protect those I care about isn't going to make sense to her. Her world is still black and white. Nuance hasn't made its way into her realm of possibilities, and it's going to be a harsh wake up call.

I hate that this is going to hurt her too.

She's going to hate me for a while, and I get it. I'll be

the bad guy. Someday she'll come to realize that I did what I had to do. Hopefully that day comes sooner rather than later, but it is what it is. I'll just have to deal with it.

So, how do I do that? How do I show up to rehearsal tomorrow with my heart frozen solid and my mind a runaway train? How do I concentrate on anything with Tess merely feet away from me? Probably hating me. Fuck, how do I ever see her again without wanting to take it all back? I don't know if I can do it.

I turn on a playlist and grab a beer. It's too fucking quiet in here, and I need to drown out my thoughts. I can't get Tess's sad eyes out of my head; the way she looked up at me when I told her it was over yanks at my soul and wants to tear it to shreds.

Was she considering ignoring the stories in the press? Was she believing me after I told her the truth? No. That's wishful thinking on my part. She was probably just pissed that I ended it for good before she got a chance to say the words. I beat her to it.

No. Tess isn't petty like that.

The beer is cold going down, but it does nothing to soothe the fire coursing through me. My anger at the world is becoming all-consuming.

Fuck it.

I guess it's time for me to be an asshole again. Cycle back to my old defenses of not giving a shit about anything. Except Charlie. That doesn't change. I protect me and mine at all costs.

The question is, what is that cost? Who pays the price for this? Me? Or Tess?

Me. It's definitely me.

forty-one
lovely

Tess

As I step numbly back into my apartment, I don't even have a chance to process what just happened. Not a second to wrap my head around the events of the last fifteen minutes. My phone rings. It's Eliza, wanting to know what I'm doing about the latest bombshell that just detonated.

I'm as honest as I can be with her and tell her that I need to investigate it more. I'll need to monitor social media for the next few hours to see what fans are engaging with and analyze mentions and posts to get an idea of what their sentiments are. Come morning, I'll have a better idea of what we'll need to do.

It's always best to wait things like this out anyway. They can either blow up or blow over on their own with no action necessary. Two stories in a row like this, in one news cycle, can go either way. It's now just a waiting game.

We agree for me to go to the office tomorrow instead

of the rehearsal space to go over things and plan our strategy. That works for me. I won't have to face Brad. Or Charlie.

My heart clenches at the thought of her discovering I'm not there tomorrow. I wonder briefly if Brad is going to tell her that we're no longer together, and how she'll take it.

But before I let my heart run away with me, I stop it. I take a deep breath, ignoring the beautiful fragrance from all the flowers still scattered around my apartment, and steel myself to the task at hand. My job. If I throw myself into my work, this won't hurt so much. If my defenses are strong enough, I won't feel anything.

I won't feel the crushing weight of the pain that's pressing down on me. I won't burst into tears like I want to so badly. I'll stop shaking from somewhere deep in my bones.

I'll survive.

I don't have an office at the label headquarters, so I set up in a conference room while I wait for Eliza to come in. I'm early and haven't slept a wink. All night, I went down the rabbit hole of posts related to Brad and his past relationships. Not just the ones with Sierra and Gina, and the current situation, but everyone he went public with. One thing stood out to me that was surprising – he never talked bad about any of them to the press. Regardless of what they did to him to end the relationships, he always had either decent things to say, or in the alternative, said absolutely nothing.

That says a lot about him as a person. Lord knows, if I were to put out a public comment after my break ups, I'd have a thing or two to say about how shitty some of my exes were. I'd shout it from the top of Tower Records, for God's sake, just to warn other women. Not Brad. He'd rather say nothing at all than disparage someone.

Even last night, when he was explaining what happened with Sierra, he didn't call her names, or curse her in any way. He just seemed lost as to why she would do what she did. I would probably strangle somebody that did that to me, but instead of acting out, he withdrew. From me.

Eliza comes into the conference room, her tall frame as graceful as ever. Her long platinum hair has green ends now, instead of her typical blue, and I wonder why the change in hue. A lot of women I know change their hair color when a major life event happens – Ivy is a prime example of that – dying her long locks when her mood shifts. I'm not that brave.

"You haven't slept, have you?" she asks, her studious eyes examining me closely. I squirm a little under the scrutiny, not wanting to give too much away.

"No. I figured this was too major to put off until this morning and wanted to get ahead of things." It's the truth anyway. She doesn't need to know the details of how derailed I got in the process.

"Okay," she huffs with a nod, tossing a notebook and

pen on the table, and sitting across from me. "Let's hear it. What do we need to do?"

"Nothing," I say, confidently.

She waits for a beat.

"Okay, go on."

I love that she's willing to hear me out on this. Eliza is a smart woman. She's in her position with Blackmore because she has good instincts. Hiring me is hopefully another one of her good decisions.

"*Blindsided* made a mistake, releasing both stories in the same news cycle. They've oversaturated social media, and confused readers to the point that they don't care."

"Well, don't we *want* people to care?" Eliza asks, resting her chin on her fists, giving me her full attention.

"We do. But not about this." I lay my tablet on the table between us to show her a few posts from fans that highlight my point. "From the metrics I've been following, general sentiment is that fans don't believe either story."

She scrolls through the posts, reading comments as she goes, and even chuckles at a few of them. "Ha. *'Blindsided, back on their bullshit again.'* Well done, sir."

"The fans are doing our job for us on this," I say, wanting to make sure she understands my reasoning. "If we make a statement, or rebuke the articles in any way, it gives them value. It shines a spotlight on them that isn't even there."

"So, why did it seem like such a big deal last night?" she asks, pushing the tablet back across the table.

"Well, for one thing, we've all got alerts for anything

related to Chaos Fuel. We're going to see things like this instantly. We're too close to it to see the full picture." I swallow hard, trying not to think about how close I am to it all.

She narrows her eyes at me, and I get the sense that she is seeing the full picture. Recent scars and all. "So, you stayed up all night, just to come in here and tell me to do nothing." It's not a question; more of a statement.

"That's my job, isn't it?" I force myself to stay professional, despite wanting to break down from the emotional exhaustion about to wash over me. Hours upon hours of seeing Brad's pictures with his exes hardened me for a while. And even putting together the metrics to show Eliza buffered me from the oncoming onslaught. But I'm starting to bow under the pressure, and Eliza's keen gaze only makes it harder to control.

"It is," she finally says, gathering her things to leave. She gives me a decidedly approving nod. "Good work. Now go home and get some sleep. You've obviously earned it."

When she's gone from the room, my body almost gives in right then. She's right. I do need sleep. There's only so much a person can take in one day, and I've reached my limit.

My life is in total chaos, but at least this is now under control. The scandal that's not even a scandal will blow over. From my years of professional experience in dealing with things like this, I know that it will.

My heartbreak? I think that one is going to be forever.

forty-two
let me leave

Brad

Sleep was not my friend last night. I spent most of the time doom scrolling on my phone, reading every horrible thing the internet had to say about me. It's a humbling experience to say the least. Needless to say, my playboy image is fully intact thanks to Sierra and Gina. If I needed anything to confirm my decision to end things with Tess was the right thing to do, that was it. She has no business getting involved with someone like me.

I drag my ass to rehearsal, as close to being fashionably late as possible, dreading seeing Tess in person, and even more so Charlie. I'm not in the mood to deal with more pain and disappointment. I have enough of my own, thanks.

When I walk in, however, there's no Tess, but Charlie comes barreling into me for an excited hug. She chatters on about her surprise sleepover last night, and I nod and comment where I can, but all I'm feeling is anxiety.

Seeing her so happy right now is killing me, because I know I'm going to have to ruin that for her. Something I've apparently become very good at.

When she finally talks herself out of breath, she yanks on my shirt, her wide gray eyes equally anxious. "Did you talk to Tess, Daddy? Did you tell her that you're sorry?"

Fucking hell. I can't do this right now.

"We'll talk about it later baby girl, okay?" I smooth a stray lock of curly hair from her face.

"But did you guys make up?"

"I said later." I'm trying to be firm without being an asshole. That's the goal, right? Be an asshole to everyone *but* Charlie?

"Mr. Summer said that Tess is at the office today, so she won't be here. I just wanted to see-"

"Not now, Charlotte." It's too harsh. Too mean. And I know it the instant I say it. I'm caught between relief and disappointment that I won't see Tess. It's fucked up.

Her expression melts from hopefulness to sadness, and my heart squeezes. The gazes of everyone else in the space bore into my back, obviously reacting to my harsh tone. Even over the loud music pumping through the room, everyone could probably hear me. I'm already failing at not being a dick to my own daughter, when that was the one thing I swore I wouldn't do.

Fuck me, I can't do anything right.

I squat down to her level, looking her in the eyes. She deserves to know the truth, but not right now. There's a time and place for this discussion, and it's not here at this moment.

"Sweetie, I did talk to Tess last night, and I'll tell you all about it later. But right now, I need to get to work, okay?"

I silently pray that I can get through this fucking day without losing my shit. And without losing my daughter. She's going to hate me when she finds out what I've done, but she can't understand all of it.

Her gaze drops, and she's chewing on a thumb nail nervously, rocking a little from foot to foot. She's not the most patient of little girls. In fact, she normally has zero patience, and is still in an instant gratification phase. When she wants something, she wants it NOW. Waiting to talk about this is going to drive her batty until it happens, but it can't be helped.

"Okay..." she finally says quietly, then twirls on a heel and heads back to Hayley and June in the corner.

Disaster averted. For now.

Ian comes over and pats my shoulder. "You doing alright there? You look a little completely exhausted."

I shake my head and smirk. "A little completely? Sounds about right."

"Well, we'll make it a short day today. Then maybe you can get some rest and, I don't know, change clothes?" He gives me a once over, and it's then that I realize that I'm wearing the same shit as yesterday. I just fucking rolled out of bed and into the car to come here, not even thinking about it.

I glance down at myself, more to avoid his gaze than anything else. "Well, fuck. Yeah...that might be a good idea."

"No worries," Ian chuckles. "We'll get you sorted."

Sorted. What a polite way to say, *'get your shit together.'* Leave it to a Brit to say that in the nicest possible way.

He's not wrong, though. I definitely need to get fucking sorted.

I'm able to get us home after rehearsal without incident, as Charlie's still prattling on about a joke that Hayley told earlier in the day. I'm half paying attention, and half lost in my own thoughts.

Practice was a fucking disaster. I kept missing cues, fucking up words, and just generally was a horrible mess. I couldn't concentrate for shit. And when we got to Dakota's new song, I nearly lost it. The words hit me differently today, they hit home. Straight in the fucking heart. I barely got through it. Nobody said anything about any of it, but I could tell from the sideways glances they were making, thoughts were being had.

I'm in the middle of flipping a grilled cheese sandwich for Charlie's lunch when she perches herself at the kitchen table, hands knotted together like she's about to give a speech.

Here we fucking go.

"Okay. It's later," she announces. All business.

I knew it. I knew we'd get here, and I'd have to do

this. It's probably best if I just come out with it. Rip it off like a bandage.

"Tess and I broke up," I say, not looking at her, and keeping my focus on the pan on the stove, the smell of melting cheese permeating the kitchen.

Silence.

I'm forced to look over and see what Charlie's doing, and find her sobbing quietly into her hands, her shoulders shaking violently.

Fuck. Fuck. Fuck. No.

I slide the pan back and shut off the burner, rushing over to Charlie and pulling her into a hug. What's left of my heart shatters even more and turns to dust in my chest. I can't breathe.

"Why?" she wails, looking up at me, her face red and streaked with tears. I do my best to wipe them away, but they won't fucking stop. *They won't fucking stop.*

"Baby girl, I know this hurts. Believe me, it hurts me too. But there are some things you're just too young to understand."

Her breath hitches, but the tears keep coming, and now confusion clouds her usually bright eyes.

"But you love her," she says between hiccups. "And she loves you."

"Baby—"

"No, Daddy. It's true. And that's all that matters."

My chest clenches. She's right about me. I do love Tess. I came to that realization last night. But she's wrong that it's the only thing that matters.

"Sometimes, loving someone isn't enough." And

don't I know it? I'll never be enough. My past will always haunt me.

Her brow furrows, but the tears keep coming. "No. You two love each other, and Mom says that if two people love each other, they can do anything."

Damn it Ren. Putting ideas like that into Charlie's head. Just because she got her fairy tale ending with Jude, doesn't mean the rest of us get that. I'm living proof we don't, no matter how much I wish it were the case.

"Not always."

"Why not? Did you even try?" The accusatory tone in her voice strikes a chord in me. A raw place that was vulnerable to the attack.

"It's complicated. Like I said, when you're older—"

"Did you try, Daddy?"

The knife twists. She's zeroed in on the heart of the matter, and all I want to do is shut down. End this conversation. Run away to another fucking country. Change my name. Anything to get out of talking about this.

My little girl is breaking this entire thing down like an expert mathematician solving an equation. And I can't respond. I can't find words to argue her straightforward logic. How could I when somewhere deep down, I know she's right?

"You're happy when you're with Tess," she whispers, the tears now slowing down. She's shifted into convincing mode, and I recognize it, but open myself to it. I *want* to be convinced. "When you smile around Tess, you get little wrinkly lines around your eyes." She reaches up to draw on my face with her finger. "You don't get those with anyone else."

"Oh, yeah?" I say. Words are still escaping me. I've been standing on a precipice, not afraid of falling, but of crushing someone else in the process. Tess. I don't want to hurt her anymore.

"Yeah. And Tess gets them too. I see them."

I scratch at my beard, considering everything. Tess's last words to me have been echoing and bouncing around my brain since last night.

"Please don't do this."

It was quiet, but I fucking heard it. And I ignored it like the selfish asshole I am. And it's plagued me ever since. After everything, she didn't want to end things. She was willing to work through it. And I just threw it all away, trying to be a martyr or some shit. Trying to save her from me.

Who the fuck do I think I am?

Do I really think I'm the end-all be-all of men? Some noble bastard saving helpless women from themselves and their poor choices in men? If Tess thinks she can handle me and all the bullshit that comes with it, shouldn't I respect her choice in me? Have some sort of faith that she can handle it? Who am I to question it?

"Please don't give up, Daddy."

I gaze into my baby girl's eyes, seeing so much hope there that it kills me. I have to fight back my own tears, and my throat tightens, nearly choking me. I would do anything to keep that hope alive in her. I will not be the one to douse this little girl's fire. It helps that I agree with her.

I was giving up on myself.

I don't want to give up on Tess.

"Okay."

forty-three
the reason

Tess

I t feels like I just closed my eyes when I'm awakened
by loud knocks on the front door. Persistent knocks.
And from the sounds of it, more than one person. My
heart starts racing, thinking there's some sort of emer-
gency. Maybe a fire in the complex. *My neighbor has cats*,
is my first scattered thought.

I scramble out of bed, barely avoiding stumbling into
the closet door in the hallway in my haste. My mind
starts racing, trying to conjure an inventory of my things,
and what I'll grab first if I get a chance to save anything.

After fumbling with the locks, I finally swing the
door open and find Brad.

And Charlie.

What the hell?

"Hi, Tess. My dad wants to talk to you," Charlie
announces as she walks past me into the apartment, and
parks herself on the couch, grabs the remote, and turns
the TV on to cartoons. I watch this in amazement as she

makes herself at home, kicking her shoes off, and curling her legs underneath her. She even grabs the throw blanket and snuggles into it, getting all sorts of comfortable.

"Hi, Charlie..." I mutter, still getting my bearings. My brain hasn't switched off the idea that there's a fire, and I'm in danger. And good thing. I'm very much in danger. Or am I still sleeping? Is this just a dream?

I pinch my arm to make sure I'm awake, and it hurts. Yup. This is real.

"You okay?" Brad asks, and I suddenly remember he's here too. When I turn back to him, still in the doorway, he looks just as tired as I feel. Dark circles shadow his stormy eyes, and I want to reach up to wipe the tiredness away. But I know I can't do that. Not anymore.

He's not mine.

"What are you doing here?" I ask, sidestepping his question. He doesn't get to ask how I'm doing.

I'm not his.

"I came to talk to you." Beneath the exhaustion, I sense fear, and I wonder what on earth he could be afraid of. He hasn't made a move to come in, and I haven't moved either to allow him to. "Please, Tess. Let me make this right."

Make this right? How does he think he can do that? He broke my heart and stomped on it right in front of me. There's no way to fix that.

"He wants to tell you he's sorry for being a jerk," Charlie says from behind me, and when I glance back, she's still glued to the TV, but obviously very aware of what's happening.

"So, this is a tag team thing?" I ask Brad, planting a hand on my hip. If he's using Charlie to get me back, that's low, even for Brad. Especially after showing how protective he is over her.

"No, not at all," Brad reassures. "But Charlie did set me straight on a few things. Which is why I'm here." He rakes a hand through his hair and my fingers twitch with memory of how it felt to do the same thing. How soft the strands were sliding through my fingertips. "Can we talk?"

I study him closely, debating internally whether to see this through. I've barely had time to digest last night's devastation personally and not just professionally. I'm not sure I'm ready for anything new. But something in his eyes makes me want to listen to whatever he has to say. A spark that always draws me in to him. It's that cosmic magnetic pull between us that I could never deny.

And I can't deny it now, either.

Without a word I step back, lowering my gaze slightly to invite him in. When he slides past me, his cologne follows, enveloping me in all things Brad. On top of the room still full of flowers, it's a bit overwhelming.

Still silent, I lead Brad through the sliding door to a small square patio surrounded by a tall privacy fence. There's barely room for two chairs and a rarely used gas grill, but it will do. We each take a seat, our knees almost touching. It's only now I realize how disheveled I must look, having just jumped out of bed. Nervously, I try to fix my hair, and wipe under my eyes to clear any stray mascara. Not that any of it matters, but it makes me feel a little more awake.

Before I can completely pull myself together, Brad grabs my hands, forcing me to look right at him. The suddenness of it jolts me, and I can't look away.

"I'm a selfish asshole," he says, but then stops. Obviously searching for what else to say.

"This is me not arguing with you," I say flatly. Despite my wretched state, I do have my full wits about me now at least.

His lip twitches like he wants to laugh, but he controls it, serious again. "I mean it. I thought I was doing the right thing last night, breaking things off. Protecting you from the bullshit of my past that always finds a way to haunt me. But I wasn't protecting you. I was protecting myself."

"I don't understand. You broke up with me to protect me?"

He squeezes my fingers, pulling me a little closer. "That's what I thought I was doing, but that's not reality."

"And what's reality?"

He sighs and lowers his gaze to our hands. "The reality is that I was ashamed and full of guilt. For anything related to me to hurt you like that...I just couldn't handle it. Not only did I not want to do that to you ever again, but I hate being the cause of it."

"None of that was your fault..."

"Isn't it, though?" He meets my eyes again, and the

anguish there punches me in the gut. "I'm not a perfect person. I never have been. And shit like yesterday with Sierra and Gina is probably going to happen again. Hell, Tess, our first date was a fucking shitshow with Gina fucking showing up like that. I may not control any of it anymore, but I am certainly the cause of it. If it weren't for me, and who I used to be, you wouldn't have been so hurt yesterday."

"Brad..."

"No, see, here's the thing," he looks away, focusing on something off in the distance. "Regardless of the circumstances of what happened, there was something in your mind that allowed you to believe the worst about me. Right?"

He shifts to look at me, and I squirm a little. He's absolutely right. Instead of giving him the benefit of the doubt, I believed right away that he was the kind of person who would betray me. That's on me.

Now it's my turn to look away, but I force a nod, ashamed of myself to admit it. I did think the worst.

"I don't blame you, Tess. Not even a little bit. If I were in your shoes, I would have believed it too. But see, I did that to myself. I have fucked up my reputation in such a way that I made it so fucking *easy* for you to believe it. That is what I'm ashamed of. And the guilt I have for the shitty life I've led, leading up to you, the one person I *want* to believe in me, was overwhelming. So, I pushed you out and ran away like a fucking coward."

Tears sting and prick the back of my eyes. I can't stand seeing him like this. "You're not a coward."

"Yes, I fucking am. And I'm sorry." He pulls on my hands, forcing me to face him again. It hurts me deeply to see so much turmoil on his face. His whole body is tense with emotion. "I'm sorry, Tess. I truly am."

"I'm sorry too," I whisper, my voice cracking. "Am I dreaming this right now? Am I still asleep? Are you real?" My hands slide out of his and reach for his face, my fingers dragging along the scruff on his chin.

He grabs onto my wrists, firmly planting me in reality as a grin spreads on his lips. I love that smile. The one that reaches his eyes when he's truly happy. I want him to smile at me like that all the time.

"Yes. I'm real," he chuckles, but then grows serious again, his voice husky, making the hairs on the back of my neck stand on end. "Tell me you forgive me."

"I forgive you."

"Tell me we're not over."

"We're not over."

"Tell me you love me."

"I love you." I say it without thinking. It's automatic. It's true.

His brows raise in surprise at my admission, but the smile is back. "Good. Because I happen to love you too."

My own smile grows. For a second, my mind played tricks on me that this was just a joke to get me to say it. The three words that are the easiest and hardest to say: *I love you*. But when he says it back, I know it's true. I feel it in my soul.

Brad Fucking Chambers loves me.

He leans in slowly, hesitating to read my face once more. "You're sure?"

"I'm sure."

"Absolutely?" he gets closer, his warm breath tickling my lips.

"Absolutely," I say with a nod, anticipation of his kiss sending shivers through me.

"Without a doubt?" he asks, millimeters away now.

"Without a—"

I don't get to finish because he brushes the words away with his lips, teasing me with the softest of kisses. It takes my breath away, it's so sweet.

He pulls back slightly to look me in the eyes, his stare hard and full of passion. "I do love you, Tess. We've only known each other a short time, but I don't need more time to know how I feel. The last twenty-four hours without you were too much. I don't want to do that again."

"Same," I say, swallowing hard. His words are like lyrics to a new favorite song. One that I will replay over and over again.

He kisses me again, and this time we let our emotions run free just a little bit more. His tongue drawing mine in to meet his, slow and smooth, and perfect. His hand cups the back of my head gently holding me to him, keeping me steady. It's a kiss that transcends everything behind us, laying his past and mine to waste, giving only a promise of the bright future ahead of us.

A future we're going to face together.

"Aww. Good job, Dad!" Charlie's voice rings from

right next to us. We both jump apart quickly, not having heard the door slide open.

"Charlie! Hey...baby girl," Brad exclaims, smoothing his beard nervously, his face reddening. He clears his throat loudly. "Didn't hear you sneak up on us..."

"I didn't sneak. You just didn't hear me."

I guess we can't argue that logic. My heart was racing so hard, I probably wouldn't have heard a plane crash on the other side of the fence either.

Brad nods while smiling at me. "Point taken."

She climbs up on Brad's lap, hugging his neck. Eyeing me carefully, she asks, "Did you two make up?"

I love what a straight shooter she is. I hope she never loses that.

"We did."

"Good. I told my dad that when two people love each other, they can do anything. Isn't that right, Dad?"

"That's right, baby."

My heart swells, and I'm overcome with emotion. Maybe I'm still exhausted. Or maybe I just realized how important the two people in front of me have become, and how much I care about them. And how lost I'd be without them in my life.

Even in our short time apart, when the world felt like it was coming to an end, I felt their loss deeply. They've become a part of my daily life now. The thought of another day without them was positively devastating.

I don't ever want to feel that way again.

Ever.

We spend the evening together, watching old cartoons and eating popcorn, Charlie snuggled happily between us, holding the bowl. Brad rests his arm along the back of the couch and plays with my hair. It's hypnotizing and could probably put me to sleep if I let it.

When I dare to glance over at him, I find him staring at me, his eyes thoughtful, and a dreamy smile on his lips. He looks happy. Relieved. Tired. And, if I'm not mistaken – in love. With me.

I grin back at him, letting him know I feel the exact same way, then toss a piece of popcorn at him. He deftly maneuvers to catch it in his mouth without jarring Charlie, who I think is now sound asleep. It is getting late. The evening together flew by, but I don't want it to end.

"Stay the night?" I ask Brad quietly. "I don't have another bedroom, but the couch—"

"Yes, please." He doesn't whisper or even attempt to be quiet.

"Shhh. You'll wake Charlie," I hiss, shifting to get up without disturbing her too much.

"Nah. She sleeps like the dead once she's out," he says, getting up with me and tucking the blanket around Charlie's small frame. "Just keep the TV on low in case she wakes up, so she doesn't forget where she is. She's kind of used to traveling and waking up in weird places, so it's cool."

I'm not sure if I should be impressed at Charlie's ability to sleep anywhere, but I think I am. I have trouble sleeping in strange hotels when I travel for work, and I'm not looking forward to the upcoming tour and the lack of sleep that will come from it. Actually, I haven't thought much about the tour...or the sleeping arrangements...

"Does this mean I get the bed...? With you?" Brad asks, arching a sly brow and sliding a hand around my back.

"It does..." I smile, grabbing that hand and leading him down the hall to the bedroom.

Once inside, Brad closes the door, but then pulls it barely open so not even a sliver of light peeks through.

"We'll have to be quiet, though," he says, stepping up to me and resting his hands on my hips. Just his closeness is enough to turn me on. Never mind the muscles, the tattoos, the cologne, the hair, the face...the *everything* about the man in front of me. "Can you be quiet?"

I can't help the shiver that lets loose.

"I can be quiet."

"Oh yeah? What about when I do this?" He pulls on my hips and grinds into me, his erection pressing in just the right place to make me gasp. "Now, now. You said you'd be quiet."

"Sorry," I breathe, my skin coming alive under his touch as his hands run up my back, undoing my bra. His calloused fingers play expertly with my nipples. He trails hot kisses down my neck and along my collarbone and my breath inhales sharply again as electricity shoots through my core.

I can feel him smile against my shoulder, and can

picture how deliciously wicked it is, and it revs me up more.

"What about you?" I whisper, dragging my tongue lightly along the hollow of his throat. "Can you be quiet?" I slide my hand between us and into the front of his jeans. His hard length twitches as I wrap my fingers around it firmly.

He lets out a low groan, pushing into my hand. My back arches instinctively at the sound, my body hungry for him.

"Careful...we need to be quiet, remember?" I tease, pumping him slowly. My own grin wicked.

I've never been intimate with someone when a child was just in the other room, and something about it makes it feel naughty, or off-limits. Like we're about to do something really taboo, even though it's totally not.

He quickly pulls my hand from his cock and walks me backward. The moonlight from the bedroom window silhouettes his lithe body as he lowers me gently to the bed, then slides in next to me.

This is where we shine. Giving each other pleasure. And every time we're together like this is like a rediscovery of the other's body. But at the same time, it's instinctively familiar. Something about this feels different, though. This feels more important now. Sweeter and deeper somehow that I can't explain.

His fingers running gently along my bare skin feels reverent, as if he's worshipping my body. Goosebumps rise in his wake with every caress, every kiss.

And when he glides into me smoothly, my leg over

his hip, we're side by side, and eye to eye. Completely connected in every way. I'm almost overcome with emotion yet again because I can see every one of his.

His sorrow, his relief, his joy...his love. It's all there on full display for me to bear witness to.

"I love you, Tess," he whispers, and the awe in his voice nearly pushes me over the edge. I had no idea that true love would make this even better than before. Because before was pretty fucking great.

I can't form words, and as we rock together slowly, both of us building to an ultimate climax of earth-shattering proportions, I kiss him. With every fiber of my being, I pour all of my love and passion into him. Eager to show him just how much I love him right back.

Each movement of our bodies is perfection, our skin slick with sweat from the heat and tension between us. And as we crescendo into pulsing ecstasy, we both break the kiss, gasping for air.

"Shhh," he chuckles, burying his face into my pillow.

"Hush yourself," I giggle softly, pulling him closer to me as he continues to thrust slowly, driving me crazy.

The fact that we can go from inferno-hot teasing, to emotionally loaded lovemaking, to now giggling about making too much noise is exactly what I love about this man. He's not just one thing. He's many. And I love all of them. All of him.

I absolutely love every single bit of him.

epilogue

I Only Wanna Be With You
Brad – Two months later

I can't believe I'm here. Our usual family restaurant with my two best girls with me. Hell, even our regular server Lauren is back. It's just like old times.

Chaos Fuel just got back from our very successful tour of the southwest, and this is the first we're seeing Charlie since our return. Tess has been bouncing off the walls, anxious to see her since we got into town last night. The video calls with all of us while we were on the road just weren't enough. A simple dinner together, with movies to make fun of on tap for later sounds like the perfect way to reunite after being apart.

"Well, if it isn't the cutest couple in the world," Lauren says to me and Tess, then gives Charlie a wink. *And that just earned her a huge tip.*

"Yup," Charlie crows, very proud of herself for orchestrating the entire thing. To be fair, I don't know if we'd be here today without her running interference for us. "We're on a date. Well, *they* are."

Tess blushes and says to Lauren, "It's not a date..."

"What are you talking about?" I say, pulling her closer next to me. "Every time I'm with you it's a date." I nuzzle my face into her neck, making her squeal with laughter, and hopefully embarrassing her even more. She hates it when I do this in public. At least she says she does. I know she secretly loves it. And honestly, I can't help it.

Both Charlie and Lauren laugh at my antics, and I know my work here is done.

We catch up on all things Charlie, and what hell she's been raising while we were gone. Apparently, her younger brother, August, has taken to following her around incessantly. This is also, apparently, very inconvenient for her.

"I mean, I'll be in my room by myself reading, and he just storms in without knocking. Bugging me constantly." She huffs loudly and crosses her arms over her chest, obviously put out about the whole thing.

"But he's your little brother. He just wants to spend time with you," Tess coos with sympathy. "You guys were apart for a long time. He probably missed you terribly."

Charlie lifts a shoulder as if she doesn't care, but I can see a lip twitch in satisfaction. The she devil. She loves the attention from August, I'm sure. I'm also pretty sure she loves *this* attention too.

Oh, to be a kid again, when all you wanted was attention. What a wild world I'm in now I have that attention as the singer in a kind of popular band, all I seek is the privacy of moments like this with the people I care about.

I am not the same person I was a decade ago. And thank God for that.

My life has changed so much. Especially since meeting Tess. She's changed my world for the better. Things that used to matter, stupid shit – like my past, don't mean a damn thing anymore. What matters is *now*.

This.

This is what matters.

Yes, my music, the band, my career, they're all important, but if they were taken away tomorrow, I could probably move on. So long as I had Tess by my side, I would be fine.

We would be fine.

The strangest thing is that I'm enjoying the music more now. For a while, it was getting to be a drag...a chore...a fucking job, and I was starting to resent everything about it.

Somehow, I've been set free to be creative again, and writing with Dakota is fucking off the charts. We've become some sort of dynamic duo of songwriting, and I love it.

He's still got his dark moments. We all do. But he works through it, and we all support him as best as we can.

Tess has indeed changed my life, and in turn, it's changed everyone's lives for the better. And it's not just our public image that's improved since she came along, though, admittedly, that's huge. The whole Sierra and Gina things were eventually found out to be bullshit as she predicted, and everything blew over like she said they would. And nobody from my past has fucked with us since. I doubt anyone will now.

Everything has gotten better.

Touring and being on the road are still a grind, but we've all clicked in a way that Chaos Fuel never has before.

We've leveled up.

Fuck. Maybe we've just *grown* up.

Well...It's about fucking time.

THE END

mayhem playlist

https://rebrand.ly/0gnmouf

1. Sleep Theory, *Numb*
2. Halestorm, *Rock Show*
3. Joey Ramone, *What A Wonderful World*
4. The Go-Go's, *This Town*
5. Savage Hands, *Love No More*
6. Lifehouse, *Hanging By A Moment*
7. Thousand Foot Krutch, *Down*
8. The Wombats, *Turn*
9. Sick Joy, *Dissolve Me*
10. Kim Wilde, *Boys*
11. Black Math, *Strangelove*
12. Gates, *Where To Begin*
13. Hoobastank, *Lucky*
14. PVRIS, *Only Love*
15. SLAVES, *Warning From My Demons*
16. Debbii Dawson, *Terrified*

17. Ufo ufo, *Strange Clouds*
18. The Temper Trap, *Sweet Disposition*
19. Evans Blue, *Say It*
20. Crown the Empire, *Blurry*
21. Audioslave, *Be Yourself*
22. Digital Daggers, *Still Here*
23. Sleep Token, *Chokehold*
24. Art Of Dying, *Falling*
25. Sleep Token, *The Summoning*
26. Hey Violet, *Like Lovers Do*
27. Loveless, *Middle of the Night*
28. Hesta Prynn, *Beside Myself*
29. Joseph Vincent, *Pillowtalk*
30. Volbeat, *The Bliss*
31. Holding Absence, *A Crooked Melody*
32. Rain City Drive, *Prayers*
33. K. Flay, *Four Letter Words*
34. Friday Pilots Club, *Life Support*
35. Catch Your Breath, *Shame On Me*
36. Caskets, *Lost in Echoes*
37. SLAVES, *True Colors*
38. SLAVES, *I'd Rather See Your Star Explode*
39. Bad Omens, *Said & Done*
40. Rain City Drive, *Like I Do*
41. Billie Eilish (with Khalid), *Lovely*
42. Currents, *Let Me Leave*
43. Gatlin, *The Reason*
44. Volbeat, *I Only Wanna Be With You*

If you enjoyed this book, please consider taking a moment to leave a review. Even a star rating helps indie authors reach a wider audience.

goodreads   amazon kindle   BookBub

also by amy booker

Near Miss Rock Star Series

Almost

So Close

Barely

Near Miss Rock Star Collection

In Reach

Drive Me Wild Vegas Series

Ms. Fortune

Ms. Chief

Ms. Lead

Ms. Take

The Mischief Motors Collection

Rhapsody Rock Star Series

Coda

Reprise

Overture

Waltz

Sustain

Chaos Fuel Rock Star Series

Mayhem

contact amy

Follow

My website: http://www.amybookerauthor.com
Facebook: www.facebook.com/amybookerauthor
Instagram: www.instagram.com/amy_booker_author/
TikTok: www.TikTok.com/@amybookerauthor
Goodreads: www.goodreads.com/author/show/
22225202.Amy_Booker
Amazon: https://rebrand.ly/sraegoj

Buy Direct

Amy Booker Store: https://payhip.com/AmyBooker

Interact

Email: amybookerauthor@gmail.com
Facebook Reader Group: https://www.facebook.com/
groups/amybookersroadies
Newsletter Sign Up: https://www.amybookerauthor.
com/subscribe

Read Early

Join my ARC Team: https://forms.gle/Ns1QKmrrs
Qz4ay5S6

www.ingramcontent.com/pod-product-compliance
Lightning Source LLC
Chambersburg PA
CBHW070048030726
47506CB00002B/406

* 9 7 9 8 9 8 8 5 1 3 5 9 9 *